"A filmmaker comes to terms with his past in Southeast Asia while battling denizens of the criminal underworld in this debut political thriller ...

In a brisk succession of clipped chapters, Haggman, an advertising agency entrepreneur, incorporates vital snippets of Vietnam's past into the framework of his novel. This sense of nuance embellishes the storyline, gives readers historical perspective, and gives the nefarious evildoers a purpose for their malevolence ...

Overall, these qualities add up to a thrilling, fully immersive, and cinematic reading experience.

An impressive novel, brimming with action and history, with a lead character that has enough swagger for future adventures."

–KIRKUS REVIEWS

"What Raymond Chandler's oeuvre did for sunny, corrupt, and haunting L.A., Eric Haggman's THE APOLOGY—an effectively noirish tale—does for Vietnam ...

In the film Apocalypse Now, director Francis Ford Coppola and screenwriter John Milieus gave a panoramic view of the Vietnam War via a boat trip upriver for a rendezvous with a killing zone overseen by a crazed Special Forces colonel... The same type of panoramic view is provided by Eric Haggman ...

(continued)

Although Haggman reminds readers of the Western colonial presence that once controlled Vietnam, (Vietnamese waiters speak in French accents), he doesn't reserve his twists merely for the obligatory car chases and brutal beatings; he surprises by making The Apology not about America apologizing to Vietnam for the war they waged there, but about the guilt felt by modern-day Japanese for what Hirohito's government did to the Chinese in Vietnam during the late 30s and World War II period ...

Today, World War II is chiefly remembered for Nazi atrocities. But it is useful to remember that Imperial Japan had its own share ... The achievement of Haggman is that when he does note the setting of this fast-paced adventure novel, it meets the demands of true noir: the country is as much a character as any of the villains."

—RON CAPSHAW FOR INDIEREADER

"Is Haggman the new Patterson? The Apology is both a fast-paced adventure novel and an extraordinarily clear and accurate description of the disturbing relationship between the militaristic Japanese and their Chinese pre-war victims. Haggman is a superb storyteller with a visual sense of words who makes this disturbing era come pictorially to life."

Read it now because when it's a major Hollywood film, you and I can claim to have discovered this formidable talent."

—JAMES X. MULLEN, FOUNDER MULLEN ADVERTISING, AUTHOR OF "THE SIMPLE ART OF GREATNESS" AND COAUTHOR OF "BRIAN REDMAN: DARING DRIVERS, DEADLY TRACKS"

"With the launch of "The Apology," Haggman takes a first ambitious step toward joining the ranks of advertising creative directors turned authors whose names will be known to anyone who has ever perused the paperback shelves of airport book shops ...

We first meet (Christian Lindstrom) in his suite at the luxurious Hotel Metropole in Hanoi, a city once better known to his generation for its so-called Hanoi Hilton, infamous home to American prisoners of war. The poignancy of the contrast is not lost on Lindstrom, who even after all these decades remains in his mind a prisoner of that war in this land he swore he'd never return to ...

Delivered with the viral velocity of 21st-century social media and ingeniously manipulated to provoke public outrage, "The Apology" turns into a page-turner ...

In this whodunnit, it's hard to say who done what, as victims are revealed as perpetrators, perpetrators fall victim to their own naiveté, and Robin Hoods become mafiosa ...

When the action moves cinematically from Vietnam to Japan's neon-lit urban landscape, film buffs might also see in "The Apology" a cross between Sophia Cappola's Tokyo-centric "Lost in Translation," and the Osaka gangster-scape of Ridley Scott's 1989 thriller, "Black Rain"..."

–Joann Mackenzie, Staff Writer,
Gloucester Daily Times

A thrilling look into Vietnam and Japan

"Haggman's book is a wonderful look into the politics behind Vietnam and Japan, and **the story is a gripping thriller told at a lightning pace.** It was a pleasure to read just for the suspense, but a pure joy to get this kind of insider's look at the politics and culture of these countries from the Vietnam Conflict to today."

—ALEXANDER DOLAN,
AUTHOR OF "THE EUTHANIST"
AND "THE EMPRESS OF TEMPERA"

———

"**Fasten your seatbelts, it's going to be quite a ride!** Once you start reading The Apology, you won't want to stop. There are lots of twists and turns as protagonist Christian Lindstrom struggles with corrupt governments, the deadly Yakuza (aka Japanese mafia). He has his own demons to deal with when he returns to Vietnam to make a tourism commercial but he becomes part of a twisted plot involving love interest Nachi Tanaka ..."

—JULIA LEONARD, AUTHOR OF "COLD CASE"
LONDON, ENGLAND

———

"Asian underworld intrigue - read it! It was so interesting to read about the history, the people and the culture all wrapped up in an intriguing story about the Asian underworld.

I want to see the movie version!"

—LYNN A. ROBINSON, AUTHOR OF
"PUT YOUR INTUITION TO WORK,"
"LISTEN," "REAL PROSPERITY"

"*Five gold stars. What a great read! After the first page, I couldn't put it down. Just as I thought I knew what would happen next, there would be a surprise twist.* **What's not to like— an inside track on corrupt government officials coupled with the Japanese mafia** *and flashbacks to Christian Lindstrom's war memories make for the terrific tale. As a fellow author, I know the value of a 5 star rating. This book is getting them and it's well deserved.*"

–KIM WALLACE, COAUTHOR OF
"WHY PEOPLE DON'T BUY THINGS"

———

"*Mr. Haggman certainly did his research for the book,* **I felt that I was immersed in the setting...he painted a beautiful picture of this part of the world** *as it is now without allowing the reader to forget the harsh reality of what it was during the Vietnam War.*"

–SANDRA COLETTA, AUTHOR OF
"THE OWL APPROACH TO STORYTELLING:
LEAD WITH YOUR LIFE"

———

"*A good book is a book you can't put down. A great book is a book you want to last forever. A classic is a book that captures your mind and becomes part of your life.* **The Apology will become a classic.** *I journeyed around Asia with Christian Lindstrom and felt I was part of his complicated and dangerous world. I look forward to the movie "The Apology" starring Kevin Costner. Thank you Eric Haggman for creating a classic that has become part of my life.*"

–PATRICIA CASTRABERTI, AUTHOR OF
"THE PRINCE RESTAURANT"

THE APOLOGY

By Eric Haggman

A corrupt government,

a manipulated press,

an evil creative arm,

and a terrible secret

could decide the fate of a country.

THE APOLOGY

Copyright © 2016 by Eric Haggman

WGAW #1827502

First Edition

Library of Congress Cataloging-in-Publication Data has been applied for.

ISBN 978-0-9973137-0-3 (softcover)
ISBN 978-0-9973137-1-0 (eBook)

For Emily

My one true love

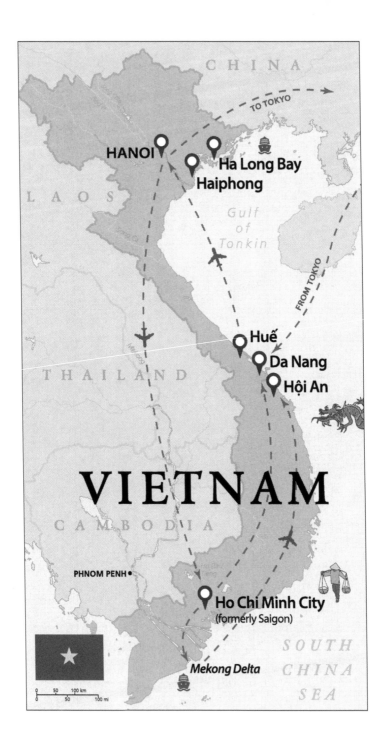

CHAPTER 1

My name is Christian Lindstrom.

I was sitting in the Charlie Chaplin Suite of the incomparable Metropole Hotel in Hanoi, Vietnam, surrounded by movie stills and pictures of the "Little Tramp" covering the walls. Following a secret marriage in 1936, Chaplin spent his honeymoon in this suite with his bride, Paulette Goddard—one of Hollywood's leading ladies at the time. Working at an antique writing desk, I was planning the next day's shot list for a Vietnamese tourism commercial and online video that we were producing for a high-end tour company specializing in big-budget, luxury tours of Southeast Asia. We were working directly for their agency, Oshima Advertising, in Tokyo.

For the next two weeks, we would be filming all

over Vietnam—from the Mekong Delta to Ha Long Bay, from Ho Chi Minh City to Da Nang and Hoi An—showcasing the best five-star-hotel properties in the country. The irony of coming back to a peaceful Vietnam, sitting in this suite dedicated to an American movie star, was not lost on me.

Two days earlier we had started the shoot in Hue. There, it had felt like I was going into a black hole, standing on the exact same street corner where we had lost six guys many years earlier.

It was a cloudless, sunny day. With me, was our Japanese-Vietnamese producer, Nachi, and our translator, tour guide, and production assistant, Hai. We were supposed to be picking out shots for the next day's shoot, but I couldn't stop crying. We were walking down the exact streets where I had fought, and the memories were coming back in waves. Not a very professional way to start a shoot. I tried to be quiet, but couldn't stop the river of tears.

We stood at the intersection where the North Vietnamese Army (NVA) had zeroed in with mortars, B-40 rockets, and recoilless rifles. Our squad had been working its way down the street. As we turned the corner, the NVA opened up on us from everywhere.

Visions of the terror, of the incredible noise: the screaming, the firing, and the huge explosions flashed before my eyes as I felt the oppressive heat and the sweet, putrid smell of death. Across the way now stood a little coffee shop where I had dragged a dying sergeant with half his head blown off. The walls of the shop were still covered with old bullet holes.

It was a relief when we left Hue for Hanoi. I'd sworn that I'd never go back to Vietnam. But when we were offered the job, I convinced myself that Vietnam was now a totally changed place with millions of different people and a thriving economy. We were shooting commercials of five-star hotels for God's sake. And I was getting $500,000 to do it. But going back to Hue, the war had come roaring back into my consciousness with a haunting fear that had no basis in fact.

Now in Hanoi, we were figuring out how to shoot the Ho Chi Minh Mausoleum where the guards were not exactly friendly; they guarded his embalmed body as if he were still alive.

The three of us headed down to the hotel's poolside Bamboo Bar. The pool was part of the Metropole's landscaped courtyard. It shimmered in a tropical blue-green light that glowed from the bottom all the way up the sides of the hotel's French-colonial-style white walls and green shuttered windows. Under the pool was the bomb shelter that had been built during the war, when we were blowing up parts of Hanoi. Now— it's a tourist attraction and part of the hotel's "Path of History" tour.

We shared a bottle of pinot grigio, ordered dim sum, and joked with the Vietnamese bartenders, who spoke English with French accents, all while making a show of mixing complicated-looking cocktails at top speed.

Nachi offered up one of her famous riddles. "What's black and white and read all over?"

"A newspaper," I kidded. "You've got to get better material. I knew that one in third grade."

The first time we worked together was in Hong Kong doing a TV shoot for the Peninsula Hotel, where Nachi's silly riddles were a main part of the entertainment. My production company had found her in a search for a producer for the commercial. I saw a picture of her on the Internet. She had high cheekbones and a pretty face with excellent production credentials from working on commercials and feature films. What I didn't find out until Nachi showed up at the airport was that she was also an absolute ten—a total bombshell.

She dressed fairly conservatively, was very well spoken, and for me—a disturbing distraction. When we'd walk around Hong Kong, people would regularly trip and fall when they saw her coming. I made a real effort not to stare at her big breasts. When I talked to her, I tried to focus on the center of her forehead in an effort to stop my eyes from wandering. Still, being around such a stunning woman made everyone feel good. She consistently projected a warmth and friendliness that made even the most mundane production planning seem interesting.

Nachi hardly ever stopped working. She scheduled the airlines, cars, drivers, hotel arrangements, and multiple shooting crews for twelve different locations. She managed the budgets, payments, transportation, meals, crew calls, shooting permits—pretty much everything, including bribes for local officials.

On the last night of the shoot, we had a big wrap party to celebrate the beautiful shots we captured—the result of working twelve hours a day together for over three weeks.

The Peninsula staged our party on the Sun Terrace overlooking Hong Kong's Victoria Harbour. It was a perfect night, watching the city's mighty laser light show flashing across the harbor. They had a good band. Nachi and I danced a lot. The party went late.

We ended up making out on a couch in Nachi's room with some terrific hugging and a little French kissing. And then she took off her sweater, followed by her big blue-and-white flowered bra. I was speechless— suddenly sitting there with my arms around this gorgeous, topless girl in a black pencil skirt.

I had dreamt about it, but was shocked that it was actually happening. It ended up being the most torrid, charming evening of my life. She was so beautiful and so much fun. But in the morning, she told me she had a boyfriend in Tokyo whom she loved. I tried not to show it, but I was crushed, like a beer can in a trash compactor ... but I never forgot her.

CHAPTER 2

The next morning, I woke up to gray overcast skies with a slow, soft drizzling rain. Hai had arranged for three rickshaw drivers to take us around Hanoi's Old Quarter, at a nice, slow speed, so that we could film the merchants and their jammed-together small shops. Nachi and Hai were armed with tiny 1080p GoPro cameras, and I was shooting with a bigger Sony digital camera that could still easily pass as a tourist's camera after taking off the shotgun microphone and lens hood.

I thought it was going to be a horrible shoot with the rain, but the footage turned out to be amazing. The drivers had rigged up plastic sheets that were draped across the top of the rickshaws to keep our cameras dry. It was so gray out that all the shopkeepers had turned on their store lights, so we got these perfect little colorized scenes of one lighted shop after another, popping out of the gray. There was a gorgeous corner flower shop filled with carnations, mums, and fragile orchids carefully wrapped in bouquets of cellophane alongside bored shopkeepers sitting on their front stoops, listening to a radio or eating a bowl of pho noodles, talking to a customer or waving to a motorbike going by.

The streets were alive with motorbikes. Like a giant mechanical ant farm, they were everywhere. Everyone was wearing helmets and rain gear, playing a full-scale, never-ending game of chicken. Somehow our rickshaw drivers seemed to magically float through the chaos, like our rickshaws had special protection.

Being a gray, overcast day didn't hurt the filming at the Ho Chi Minh Mausoleum either. The building was done in a brutalist gray-stone Russian architecture that could fit right into Red Square or double as a bomb shelter.

We gave Hai the cameras to watch, and Nachi and I got in line to see Ho's embalmed body. The guards wore white formal uniforms and peaked hats trimmed with a band of red-and-gold braiding. All of them had dead-serious demeanors and big bayonets on their automatic rifles.

Inside, Ho's body was laid out in a large glass case with guards standing at rigid attention on all four corners. Hai had told us that Ho had wanted to be cremated and have his ashes sprinkled in South, Central, and North Vietnam. But that was not to be. The Communist Party wanted him to be remembered and formally displayed in the same manner as Lenin or Mao.

Hai was in his early thirties and he was much more than just our translator and production assistant. Born and raised in Vietnam, he knew more about the history of the country than anyone I'd ever met. He told us that Ho Chi Minh was really more of a nationalist than a communist and that Ho had tried to get President Eisenhower to help, but "Ike" and the United States lined up with the French—making communism our last resort. Hai explained, "He wanted freedom and many political parties. But when he left power in 1969, the communists totally hijacked his image for their own use and propaganda."

Once back outside, we found Hai had been picked up by a Vietnamese police minder who had taken an interest in what we were doing. He was a short, little man who showed us his gaudy red and gold starred badge and started questioning us in rapid-fire Vietnamese. "What were we doing? Why the cameras? Where are we staying?" Hai translated, telling me in English what the real problem was, "He wants a bribe. It's a shakedown." We ended up giving him the equivalent of twenty US dollars wrapped in a piece of paper so it didn't look like he was extorting tourists.

Hai said, "It is our biggest problem—corruption. The cops know they can threaten arrest, so people who don't want trouble will just pay them."

Even after the payoff, the guy wouldn't leave. He seemed to enjoy harassing us, making us move back about fifty yards from the front of the tomb where the changing of the guard was starting to take place. Fortunately one of our cameras had a long lens so we were able to get some good shots of the military ballet.

The guards carried their rifles high on their chests and marched in unison with a slow, high-stepping cadence that was right out of a Russian May Day parade.

'We then moved on to shoot footage of the nearby Presidential Palace of Vietnam, completed in 1906 to house the French governor-general, who ruled French Indochina. Its French-colonial architecture was pointedly European, incorporating Italian Renaissance elements with its yellow stucco walls, red tile roof, and wrought-iron gates.

Hai gave us the history, "When North Vietnam achieved independence in 1954, it was expected that Ho Chi Minh would live in the mansion, as it was now the property of the Vietnamese government and a symbol like your White House. Ho Chi Minh refused to live in the luxurious building, where memories of France's ruling the country were all too painful. Instead he moved to a small cottage on a lake, a hundred yards from here."

We set up and filmed Ho's cottage, called "Number 54." It was more like a Vietnamese country house and hardly bigger than a two-car garage. Then Hai pointed to "Uncle Ho's Stilt House" across the lake, which they built for Ho Chi Minh when he turned sixty-eight. The two-room house's design was based on traditional Vietnamese northwestern houses. We could see the crowds at the cottage were so big that we'd never get in, so we decided to shoot the tree house on stilts from across the water.

The cop kept following us everywhere, only seeming to give up when we got back to the Metropole, which had its own private security service, with men wearing expensive-looking suits and earpieces at every entrance. Once inside we all felt safe and relaxed and headed right to the bar for a drink before packing up for Saigon, now renamed Ho Chi Minh City.

CHAPTER *3*

On our first night in Ho Chi Minh City, we went out to film the lights of the city center—setting up a camera on a tripod to get a time-lapse shot of the major intersection between Pham Ngoc Thach and Vo Van Tan, which was surrounded by brightly lit, tall office buildings and high-end luxury shops. One building had a giant poster of Brad Pitt peering down on us, modeling a TAG Heuer Swiss wristwatch. Across the street, an elegantly lit Chanel boutique displayed its wildly expensive haute couture collection.

The motorbike traffic was biblical. A light would turn green, and what seemed like thousands would come off the line with every imaginable combination of riders. Two adults, three kids, one bike—no problem.

Two adults and a dog with his paws on the handlebars looked perfectly normal. Then there was a guy driving his scooter with an entire mattress on his back, trying not to let it go airborne.

In twenty minutes we shot a lot of good footage, with tons of neon flashing lights, high-end stores showcasing $5,000 handbags, and the rivers of red that the motorbikes' taillights left in their wake. We moved up a couple of blocks and set up in front of the Saigon Opera House, a gorgeous structure built in 1897 by the French, which greeted you with two bare-breasted goddesses serving as pillars at the front doors. We watched playback on Nachi's MacBook. Because we were shooting in HD, we could check out our footage on a big screen then adjust the color and contrast right in the camera.

It was right about then that a minivan hit Hai, who was standing on the corner next to the camera. I was staring at the screen when I heard brakes screeching. We turned and watched helplessly as a tan minivan caught Hai on the arm with the driver-side mirror. He spun around and slammed against the side of the van. The minivan never stopped.

I ran over to Hai and knelt down. He was breathing.

I looked up at Nachi. "Was that an accident?"

Hai was dazed and groaning, and it looked like his arm was dislocated or broken. Right away, Nachi got on the phone and called the concierge at the Park Hyatt Saigon, and they called a private hospital that sent their own ambulance.

"The state hospitals will let you die before they have time to see you," she said.

We rode in the back of the ambulance with Hai. He was in real pain, sweating profusely but staying stoic. The EMTs were clearly worried about his arm—what he'd torn; what he'd broken. They started running an IV and gave him an injection to control his pain. Looking out across Nachi's face, with the streetlights racing by, I could not believe how fast things could go to hell—doing something as simple as shooting a commercial on a street corner.

It was a long night at Saint Mary's Saigon Hospital. The doctors went right to work checking Hai for internal injuries and broken bones. It went on for hours. He had a CT scan, an MRI and x-rays—the works. I sat and waited in a dim hospital hallway with Nachi. The walls had a pale-green cast that was enhanced by the old-fashioned tube lights, which flickered and hummed in the silence.

"Do you ever think about the Hong Kong shoot?" she asked quietly.

"All the time. How's your boyfriend? What's his name—Arashi?"

"Right, Arashi Tojo. We are no longer a couple," she paused. "I'm sorry it ended that way with us. It made me sad."

"Me too."

It was quiet for a very long time, just the sound of the AC vents high in the ceiling forcing out fresh, cool air.

"Christian, you know quite a bit about me, but I know almost nothing about you. What did you do after the war?"

I had told her about my first trip to Vietnam, flying into Saigon, straight out of infantry training, knowing nothing of what was to come. But it came. I was seriously wounded.

"It's not that great a story," I answered. "I was in a

hospital in Kyoto for a couple of months until they could get me walking again. It's funny—you were probably a little girl then living around there somewhere.

"When I got back, I was pretty fucked up—night terrors, despair, depression, the whole thing. My solution was to go to the Episcopal Divinity School. I thought they'd be focused on civil rights, helping poor people and ending the war. They were focused on none of these things. They were generally just a bunch of lightweights, modeling vestments and pontificating on theology. I dropped out before the year was over.

Nachi smiled and winked, "Yeah, hard to see you as a priest."

"I know, that's how messed up I was. Anyway, I wound up getting a freelance writing job at an ad agency, and after a year they hired me as a copywriter. Eventually, I worked my way up to creative director and started running the broadcast division—shooting all kinds of commercials.

"I ended up marrying this beautiful woman in the media department …

"But she was killed in a car accident when I was off on a shoot in South Africa."

"Oh my god, that's awful."

"It was. It kind of still is. I've had a lot of trouble leaving her behind. Felicia. Her name was Felicia Ellis."

The room was silent again, except for the hum of the air handler kicking in.

"Well, I've got a grisly secret to tell as well," Nachi confided. "I almost got married a few years ago to Arashi—you know, the one I told you about. He's a vice president at Oshima and pretty high up with his own division. We dated for over a year and he gave me a gorgeous diamond engagement ring. Then, I found out he was cheating on me with a makeup girl when I was away on a job. I immediately moved out of his apartment and did my best to disappear.

"But he stalked me. His car was parked outside of my apartment, at all hours of the day and night. Then, I'd get these strange hang-up calls from untraceable prepaid phones. He was unbelievably angry that I left him. He hated me. I was really scared of him and the police wouldn't do anything. So I just made it a point to be constantly on the road, any place but Tokyo. After a while, he finally got tired of being obsessed with me and found something else to do."

"Or someone else," I added.

"That wouldn't surprise me. He is a very powerful man at the agency with an important job. His group is called the 'Fix-It People.' They are brought in when an account is floundering, and take it over to get it back on track. 'Thought. Word. Deed.' is the Oshima company slogan. It's designed to be translated into hundreds of languages. His group is the 'Deed' part, and his motto is '*They don't pay you to do the work; they pay you to get the job done.*' They get the job done no matter how big or intractable the problem.

"I worked with him on a documentary for the Tsukiji Fish Market—the largest seafood market in the world. Over sixty thousand people work there. The market is on some really valuable land that's between the Sumida River and the Ginza shopping district. The problem was getting the whole gigantic operation to move to another location by 2017, in preparation for the 2020 Tokyo Summer Olympics. We had to convince some nine hundred wholesale dealers that moving to a new market in Toyosu was a good idea. At the start, no one was happy about it; they were all up in arms. At their location, they'd been collectively doing about $6 billion in US dollars in business every year.

"So we did this documentary about how great the new market would be. We paid a number of leading wholesalers to be in the film, praising the new market plan. The video was played on big flat-panel screens all over the market, projecting the idea that the new fish market would be a victory for wholesalers. At the start, it looked like an impossible selling job, but he got it done. I know for a fact that hundreds of vendors were paid off with mountains of cash. But that's how business works, right?"

"For some people," I conceded.

Around five in the morning, Hai was pushed out of the emergency room in a wheelchair, with his arm in a sling and loaded up on painkillers. Nachi translated what the nurse was saying. "He's dislocated his arm and bruised two ribs. He's also high as a kite."

Hai mumbled, "I have no pain," as we wheeled him out and carefully put him into a car sent by the hotel, but not before giving the hospital $3,000 US in cash.

The Park Hyatt had a wheelchair waiting for us and a couple of bellmen to help get Hai upstairs. We got him to his room, onto his bed, where he promptly passed out with his street clothes on. We took off his shoes and shut off the lights.

We had a big shooting crew coming at three in the afternoon to film the hotel at the sundown magic hour and beyond. Eight hours with forty people, makeup, wardrobe, models, dozens of production assistants, dollies, cranes, and especially lights. I had a local lighting director coming in who specialized in creating glamorous shots.

I woke up and called Hai's room to see how he was doing. He still sounded groggy but asked if we were going to be all right.

"Everything is fine, Hai, just rest."

We ended up shooting until eleven that night.

The staff at the Park Hyatt had done everything we asked, as well as giving us some things we didn't have the guts to ask for, like the best-looking waitresses, waiters, and bartenders I'd ever seen. They were young, funny, personable, and impeccably dressed in black, right out of central casting. It was like the old days when the airlines didn't care about seniority, only about having smart, attractive people doing the job. Not exactly the proper communist approach.

A lot of them were college students or graduates who valued the work for the Western connections and good money, as well as a chance to try out their English. All of them, right up to the German manager, had been born after the war. The Vietnam War had become an old history story they had only read about in school.

After we wrapped up the shoot, we had a late dinner at Opera, the hotel's Italian restaurant. It featured authentic cuisine prepared in a large open kitchen— squid-ink risotto, carbonara pizza, and tiramisu—all served by Vietnamese waiters. The restaurant was bathed in dim red light, with a narrow spotlight focused on each table.

Nachi asked, "What is your favorite movie?"

"The first *Godfather*," I said. "Hands down. The most inspiring movie ever made. It always gives me courage when I watch it. What's yours?"

"*Slumdog Millionaire*."

"I've never seen it."

"You've got to see it," she said with conviction.

"Well, okay."

We ended up watching *Slumdog Millionaire* on a pay-per-view channel in the living room of her suite. I fell asleep on the couch, waking up a couple of hours later. The living room was dark except for one table lamp by the door. The TV was still on, but the sound was turned off.

The door to Nachi's bedroom was ajar, and I could see her dark hair on the pillow. I stood in the doorway and quietly said, "Good night, Nachi," thinking she was asleep. But she wasn't, or it was enough to wake her up, because she got out of bed, wearing pink silk pajamas. She walked over and gave me a big hug and kissed me on the cheek. "Good night," I mumbled, and floated down the hall to my room. Or at least that's how it felt.

CHAPTER 5

The next morning, we packed up and were driven to Tan Son Nhut, which was an old US Air Force base that had been converted to an international airport. We boarded a Vietnam Airlines 737 and flew to Da Nang landing at yet another converted US air base. Hai was in good spirits, considering he was wearing a sling and we were stuffed into coach. Luckily it was a short flight.

A driver and a van were waiting for us when we landed. He drove south from the airport to Hoi An and The Nam Hai Resort, which wrapped around a pristine stretch of sand on Ha My Beach. Japanese investors had built it in a cost-is-no-object South Seas style, where Vietnamese chic meets cutting-edge design. Every villa had its own private, walled courtyard with a long, narrow koi pond bordered by lush, tropical landscaping protected by high, white stone walls for privacy. The compound they gave us was really made up of three houses—each with every conceivable amenity, including a swimming pool, an unobstructed view of the ocean through a forest of tall palm trees, and a butler. Not a butler on call. No, this was our own private butler, who lived right there on the premises in his own quarters, virtually 24/7. His name was Tao and he looked about eighteen. Sometimes it was a little weird, even though he was a friendly kid, because he was always lurking around, hoping we'd give him something to do. Laundry, food, wine, transportation— Tao was determined to make our stay perfect.

The luxury hotels and resorts that we were shooting all wanted high-end, international customers, so they pulled out all the stops when it came to giving us the best accommodations to live in and shoot.

In the evening, we shot the first of The Nam Hai's three restaurants—The Beach Restaurant. After nightfall, it was transformed into a five-star Vietnamese restaurant that served dinner outdoors by the ocean. The menu featured delicacies like green mango salad with crisp, fried coconut prawns, steamed fish wrapped in banana leaves topped with lotus seeds, and dumplings smothered in ginger syrup for dessert.

The restaurant was lit by torches and dramatic up-lighting which made the canopy of trees glow green. A couple of Vietnamese musicians played guitars, filling the place with music, blending with the sound of the waves. It was not hard to make the place look great. We had a small but experienced Japanese production crew, who had flown in the day before. They kept the shoot as discreet as possible while guests enjoyed dinner and the view.

After we wrapped, Nachi said she was going to get a car to take her to Hoi An to get some things at an all-night drugstore.

"At this hour?" I asked.

"Yes, it's fine. I'm just going there and back with the hotel car. Please leave the gate unlocked."

It was half past ten. One of the golf cart drivers gave me a ride to our compound. I left the front gate unlatched and headed for my house. I washed up, poured a glass of wine, and watched BBC News.

Around twelve thirty, I opened the door to see if

Nachi was back. Her house was dark. The gate was still unlatched. I called the front desk.

"My colleague went to Hoi An a couple of hours ago. She said she was going in a hotel car. Do you know where they are?" I asked.

"Sir, we were just going to call you. Your colleague was taken to a drugstore in Hoi An. She went in but never came out. The driver went looking for her, but she had disappeared."

"What do you mean 'disappeared'?"

"She was gone. She was not there. He waited over an hour. She never came back out."

CHAPTER 6

The hotel's chief of security called me after contacting the Hoi An police. I woke up Hai, pounding on his door.

"Hai, get up. I need your help. Now!" I shouted, "Get dressed; it's urgent."

We flew into town, sitting in the back seat of a hotel patrol car, blue lights flashing, feeling like we were barely touching the ground. We pulled up to the all-night drugstore, where there were already a number of uniformed cops and a detective. The detective spoke broken English, but we could communicate fairly well with Hai's quick translations. The detective said he wanted us to stay with the investigation because we were the only ones who knew her. They thought we might know something that could help them find Nachi.

But what? Why the hell would anyone want to hurt her?

We walked in as they were downloading the footage from the store's security cameras. The store looked exactly like a 7-Eleven back in the States. It was superbright, with front and side doors and an exit in the rear. Back in the break room, two cops had a big gray cabinet open, and they were watching a four-picture replay of the recorded footage.

The time counter said 10:48 p.m. and kept rolling as customers came in and out at double speed, looking exactly like a Charlie Chaplin movie. Then it came up—Nachi walking into the drugstore. They switched to slow motion and brought up a single image of her walking down an aisle.

She picked up a package in a section that sold aspirin and sleeping pills, but I couldn't tell what she held in her hand. Just then, like two hooded black clouds, two guys picked her up by the arms and perp-walked her out the back door. The guy on her right held a white handkerchief over her face. Just like that. Sharks in the water.

The cops kept playing it back and then started checking every other camera for the same time frame.

There wasn't much, just the same *hooded black clouds*.

The cops were fairly quick to get a dragnet going. They knew that an abduction of a female foreign visitor was not good news for Hoi An. They dispatched multiple teams on scooters buzzing down the three streets near the rear entrance. Unfortunately they were doing it with their flashing lights on, so you could see them coming ten blocks away. Plus there was the fact that each of the three streets had dozens of alleys off them, going every which way, creating a confusing maze.

A pack of motorcycle cops drove up and stopped in front of the drugstore. No scooters for them. These were the heavy-duty guys, on big white Japanese bikes, wearing crash helmets with faceplate-mounted radio mikes. The bikes also had saddlebags that could easily hold a good-sized submachine gun. These cops looked mean as hell. I'd seen the look before.

Hai listened to what their captain was saying to the lead detective. "He said they're going to establish a perimeter by closing off some streets. I couldn't understand the names. But they're bringing in more police to start searching house by house, expanding outward from the drugstore."

With his arm hanging in the sling, Hai looked as forlorn as I felt, standing there as the tough looking cops took off.

We joined a group of five regular cops, who were starting the door-to-door searches down the block. Their flashlight beams shone wildly as they knocked on doors and woke up residents. The alleys made it tough. They went at strange angles, only to lead into another alley, another doorway, another apartment, and another seemingly empty building.

The cops were fast and methodical, and they'd never heard of a search warrant. Their leader was using the GPS on his phone to keep track of where they were and what they'd covered. All the while, they were scaring the hell out of a lot of people, demanding to search their entire house before moving on. Crying kids, frightened old people, barking dogs.

Hai told me that they kept repeating, "We are here for your safety," in Vietnamese, over and over.

We went down a side street where the cops kept stopping people and asking if they had seen a tall Asian woman and two guys wearing black hoods. One person pointed down the street, and we ran to where it came out onto a canal, which was about forty yards across.

The canal was covered with colored Japanese lanterns strung across a bridge going all the way down the street. Red, green, blue, silver, purple—the lanterns swayed in the breeze, creating a dizzying, mirrored kaleidoscope of colors.

There were still lots of people coming in and out of the stores and restaurants but no Nachi, no *hooded black clouds*. The lead cop started talking on his handheld radio as we stood on the bridge scanning the area. Hai moved over to hear what he was saying, and then everyone started moving off the bridge and down the lantern-lit street.

"They've got the cell tower that picked up the last signal from her phone. It's a couple of blocks away."

We jogged along. A pair of the tough cops on white bikes went screaming by. The cell tower was in the middle of a small park, where they'd done a lot of work to make the tower look like a tall fir tree with hundreds of fake branches. Another group of cops came from the opposite direction, spreading out and searching the street, the sidewalk, and the grass, endlessly shining their flashlights back and forth.

They found her cell phone, or at least I was pretty sure it was hers. The kidnappers had been thoughtful enough to back over it with a car.

Near dawn, a policeman drove us back to The Nam Hai in a squad car. There was nothing else to do. I felt so depressed and empty, with a huge feeling of failure and loss. Nachi's house was still dark as I lay on my bed and focused on my breathing, trying to empty my head of thought—if only for a few minutes. I must have fallen asleep; I was awakened by my iPhone vibrating on the bedside table.

CHAPTER 7

"She's on YouTube," Hai shouted.

"What?"

"Nachi's on YouTube with a ransom demand, and it's a lot more than money."

I felt totally confused. Hai came over with his laptop and set it up on the dining table. An image slowly emerged out of the dark: sitting in front of a brick wall was a woman with a black hood over her head, her wrists duct-taped together. She was nervously holding a sheet of paper with her thumbs. A hand came into the frame and pulled off the hood. It was Nachi, eyes blinking at the bright lights, her hair a mess. She looked at the paper and began slowly, nervously speaking.

"My name is Nachi Tanaka. My grandfather was Japanese Colonel Akio Tanaka, who ordered the burning of three villages near Hoi An in 1945, resulting in the massacre of seven thousand seven hundred and fifty-nine men, women, and children. Many were beheaded after digging their own graves. My grandfather was never punished, and the Japanese government has never acknowledged the slaughter of these innocent Vietnamese people. I am being held against my will until the Japanese government admits to these crimes and makes them known to the Japanese people, instead of hiding these facts like the Rape of Nanking and many other atrocities. I appeal to the prime minister of Japan to right these wrongs. My life is in your hands."

Whereupon two hands came into the frame and pulled the hood back down over her head. The screen went black. This was no random kidnapping. They had known who she was. They had known she was here. They knew she was going to the all-night drugstore, and they'd had time to get set up to grab her.

The Hoi An cops ended up creating a command center at The Nam Hai conference pavilion—a large facility with a ballroom and numerous meeting rooms. A row of police motorcycles and Honda squad cars were parked in the midday sun, the air heavy with heat and humidity.

We sat around a conference table, with the chief detective at the far end. There were two uniformed policemen and five other men in street clothes, their shirts pulled out to cover their guns. They played Nachi's YouTube video four times in a row. Each time I hoped it would show more, but of course it was the same brick wall, the same black hood, and the same quiver in her voice.

Hai whispered a translation of what they were saying. Basically the video was untraceable, YouTube refused to take it down, and CNN had just done a short report on the abduction.

I raised my hand and started speaking, with Hai doing a Vietnamese translation every few sentences. "I think someone in the hotel had to help the kidnappers. They knew where she was going and exactly when."

I paused for the translation and continued. "The hotel operator, the hotel driver, or maybe the kid Tao, the butler, where we're staying. If I were you guys, I would grab all their cell phones and see who they've been talking to." Hai translated.

I was shocked when they nodded and started dispatching teams to track the people down. The chief detective also requested the hotel's phone records going back to when Oshima had made the original reservations.

I could feel the start of a headache coming on from going too long without food. I walked back to the compound, just as Tao was coming out of my house.

"Just freshening up." Then he asked, "Was Miss Nachi really kidnapped?"

I nodded. My head hurt. I was too tired for words.

"The police took my cell phone; they promised to give it back."

I nodded again and went inside the house to call the creative team at Oshima. They were very worried and asked for us to stay with the investigation until Nachi was found. One of them said, "Remember, you have a *blank check*. Pay the cops; set up a reward. Do whatever is necessary."

Tao came back with a tray of crackers, soft cheeses, marmalade, green grapes, and a cold bottle of Echo Bay sauvignon blanc. I thanked him and locked the door, but of course he had a key. He was too young, almost childlike, to be involved in an abduction, wasn't he? I took two Advil and lay down. I fell asleep into a deep dream.

I was in an alley in Hue, and we were getting the shit kicked out of us from three different directions. The impact of the explosions nearly knocked me down with each concussion. It was our third day of round-the-clock combat with 110 degree temperatures and 100 percent humidity. The clouds were continuous and dark. Practically every time we crossed a street, a man would get hit, then a marine would run to pull him to cover, and then that guy would get hit.

On top of everything, an order came through that we could not engage the enemy with "indirect-fire weapons" because that would endanger the historic buildings of Hue—the ancient capital of Vietnam. I couldn't fucking believe it. "No indirect-fire weapons" meant no artillery, no naval gunfire—which was right offshore—and no air support, as the rain clouds were low and constant.

We were a part of a two-company assault moving down the street toward the city's provincial building, walking behind two M-48 Patton tanks. The NVA started mortaring us, dropping explosive rounds all around us. The tank we were following stopped, and we crawled under it for cover. A mortar hit twenty feet away, spattering the tank with shrapnel. The noise was deafening, the engine rumbling, and then there were huge booms as the tank reared up as it fired.

We could see the flashes from a four-story building down the street. The M-48 boomed; the left half of the building imploded, and the flashes stopped. I was running bent over with two cases of machine-gun ammo, exhausted, going on instinct and terror. We had been trained for jungle fighting and riding helicopters but never house-to-house combat. We learned quickly that you had to take every room of every building, even though we were outnumbered ten to one.

The biggest things we had besides the tanks were two M-50 Ontos—light-tracked vehicles with six 106mm recoilless rifles mounted on either side of the driver. With high-velocity rounds, we could blow holes in walls and buildings to root them out. But we still had to throw grenades and go in and shoot them.

I could feel the fear going through my body like a paralyzing drug. Hour after hour, thinking I could die at any second had an awful effect on my nervous system—the adrenaline overload, the constant mortal fear, the impossible pain of seeing my own men dead, and the towering guilt for being glad I was still alive.

CHAPTER 8

Six hours later, I woke up to find Hai sitting in my darkened room watching the news on Al Jazeera with the volume on low.

"Do you want some coffee?" he asked, never taking his eyes off the TV.

"Sure."

"The BBC and CNN picked up the story. It's gone viral—with tens of thousands of hits. They even had a picture of Nachi's grandfather in uniform. What an arrogant-looking bastard."

I washed my face and I tried to shake off the nameless fear that had come with the dream.

We called for a golf cart and headed to the

conference center. The detectives looked haggard. All of them were either on a phone or a computer. Nobody looked up when we walked in. Eventually we were directed to Bao, the lead detective. He began speaking to us in flawless English.

"There was a real colonel who was with the Japanese occupying force, just like she said in the video. He was captured and repatriated to Japan."

Bao explained that Nachi's grandfather had a son, who eventually married a Vietnamese woman he had met while working on a power-plant project outside Hanoi. They later moved back to Japan, where Nachi was born.

He continued, saying that the Japanese Ministry of Defense said they had no record of Colonel Akio Tanaka, other than his graduation from military college and his original deployment to China in the late thirties. Bao said he kept pressing them, but they could not explain where the rest of his file had gone.

Hai told me what Bao had told them. "More Japanese lies. Fuck you. Stay out of our country."

I was amazed by Bao's abrupt anger, but as far as I was concerned, he had a right to it. The Vietnamese had been ruled by the Chinese for a thousand years, followed by the French, followed by the Japanese and then the French again, followed by the Americans. The Japanese had viewed the Vietnamese as subhuman, to be enslaved, murdered, raped, and starved to death. It was clear that Nachi's abduction had stirred up some deep and abiding feelings.

The cops had a TV sitting on a table in the middle of the room; it was tuned to NHK World, on which a Japanese reporter was doing a stand-up report with downtown Tokyo behind him—the English translation in subtitles.

"The prime minister's office has released a statement that they have no knowledge or record of the Hoi An Massacre and only have incomplete records of Colonel Akio Tanaka's service in Indochina, in what is now Vietnam. To quote the statement, 'It has long been our policy to never negotiate with kidnappers under any circumstances.'"

"What the hell," I blurted out. "Are they just going to let Nachi die?"

No one made eye contact with me.

Deflated, Hai and I walked back to the compound. I told him, "I want to film everything from now on, let's rig up the GoPro into a button cam."

The button cam was simply an extension that hooked up on the tiny GoPro's lens; it looked like the top button on the front of Hai's sport coat. Underneath his shirt, he wore a mount that was strapped to his chest. When he put on his sport coat over the mount, you could not tell the camera was there. It just looked like the top button was mismatched.

I also gave him a bag of ten small fully charged batteries that he could switch out to keep the GoPro running. Both cameras had big chips that could go for five hours each. Hai started out by filming a repeat of the report from Tokyo that NHK World was replaying.

It was around ten at night. I was tired but leery about going to sleep. I didn't want to have another nightmare—Hue in living color, the big fear, the endless hurt.

I wondered where Nachi was. I could see her face as the hood was pulled off: bewildered and clearly in fear. She could be anywhere, still in Hoi An or Hanoi or back in Ho Chi Minh City or dead for that matter.

With only a bedside lamp on, I couldn't see the front door, but heard it open. I slid out of bed and rushed towards it. Just as I got ready to smash the door back on whomever was behind it, Tao walked in carrying chocolates that he was going to put on the pillows.

"For Christ's sake, Tao, I could have hurt you."

He nervously handed me the chocolates. "I'm sorry, Mr. Christian," and quickly shut the door.

I lay in the dark for a long time, seeing Nachi's face and the intoxicating way she walked down the street in high heels and jeans, wearing a crisp white, button-down blouse with a wide leather belt. And people tripping when they saw her.

At quarter to seven the next morning, my iPhone started vibrating on the night table like there was a wild animal inside. I fumbled around and hit the button. It was Hai.

"Bao just called; there's another YouTube video."

I scrambled to get dressed as I combed my hair and gargled Listerine.

The conference room smelled of rotten takeout food and cops who hadn't showered for many hours. There was also an angry air to the room that was tangible. Everyone at the table looked pissed off. We asked Bao what was going on. He waved us over to his computer, sat down, and called up YouTube.

Nachi's face bloomed up on the screen. There was no hood; her hair was combed, but her wrists were still duct-taped together.

"I am Nachi Tanaka. I have been commanded to show you these pictures taken during the Hoi An Massacre. They were taken by a Japanese soldier who was an aide to my grandfather, Colonel Akio Tanaka. As you will see, these photos are too awful to be seen, yet I am going to show you anyway."

She slowly showed six mounted photos that were, indeed, too awful to be seen. Japanese soldiers shooting naked women in a pit that they had been forced to dig themselves. A child being beheaded. A village burning, with dead bodies lying everywhere. She held up each of the photos, her hands shaking, gripping them with her thumbs.

"Until the Japanese government acknowledges these crimes and makes them widely known throughout Japan, I am being held against my will. And if they do not respond in one week, I will be killed like the people murdered in these pictures."

Bao announced in Vietnamese, "Tell the networks we will see them in one hour. We will have a press conference on the progress of the investigation."

"Why is he doing that? What's there to say?" I asked Hai.

Hai replied, "I bet he wants to put the screws to the Japs to pressure them to acknowledge the massacre. We have known about the Hoi An story for years. The only one to survive was a five-year-old girl, who hid under her dead mother in a pit with many bodies. She escaped during the night. She was found two days later, wandering the jungle, dehydrated, and covered with bug bites. Even after they dug up the bodies, the Japanese denied everything, and when the French came back, it was swept under the rug."

We walked over to The Nam Hai's main reception building, which had a restaurant serving breakfast. Outside there were eight TV trucks with big satellite dishes on their roofs.

A smiling, personable Vietnamese girl, dressed in a traditional cream-colored *áo dài*, welcomed us brightly, even though we looked disheveled and stupid tired. She brought coffee and juice, and we ordered a

Western-style breakfast with eggs, sausage, and toast. The food helped. Hai went to the men's room to change the batteries in the GoPro so that he wouldn't run out in the middle of Bao's press conference.

Back at the conference center, reporters and camera crews were setting up in the main ballroom. The story had brought the BBC, CNN, NBC, Al Jazeera, and something like a dozen Japanese and Vietnamese news crews to The Nam Hai.

The press conference started with Bao walking on stage and standing at a podium. He was nearly six feet tall and wore a wrinkled off-the-rack blue suit. His tie was pulled up straight. He calmly eyed the cameras. There was a picture of Nachi from the ransom video projected on a large TV screen behind him. He flicked the microphone with his finger to see if it was alive. It made a thumping sound through the speakers on either side of him.

"Good morning," he said in Vietnamese. "I am Investigator Bao Tran of the Hoi An Police Department. As you know, we have been investigating the abduction and disappearance of Nachi Tanaka. It's been a difficult problem, trying to affect her release, with the Japanese government hiding and denying Colonel Akio Tanaka's record of command in Indochina. After our repeated requests made to the Japanese Ministry of Defense, we are convinced they are withholding all information about this atrocity.

"Here in Vietnam, the stories of the Hoi An Massacre have been known for decades. But the Japanese government and their prime minister continue this lie about their crimes of the past." With that, he walked off the stage.

"Holy God," I said to Hai. "No shortage of guts from Bao. Jesus, going after the Japanese prime minister like that?"

"Wow," Hai agreed.

He'd shot the whole thing from close in, standing near the podium.

CHAPTER 9

Within hours the news conference, with a voice-over translation, was playing on the international news channels. Al Jazeera was the first to pick it up, then the BBC. We watched a story from a local Da Nang station. It was all in Vietnamese. Hai said the story line was that "the Japanese murder us and lie about it."

Hai emphasized the report was "plenty inflammatory, and it will further light up the Vietnamese hatred of the Japanese arrogance."

Tao brought us a lunch of fish noodle soup and green tea. We sat in the living room and surfed through the news channels. The big deal was that the Japanese prime minister had no comment. It was as if they'd gone catatonic, frozen in the moment. Everyone in creation was running pictures of Nachi with the hood over her head alongside shots of her seventy-five-year-old grandfather in uniform.

We watched another news report. This one was from Hanoi at Nikkō Optical Devices outside the city. Hai explained that over two thousand Vietnamese employees at the plant had walked out en masse in protest at the end of their first shift. And it was doubtful that there would be enough people on the second shift to keep the Japanese factory going.

"If anything, this will get their attention." Hai explained, "A massive number of Japanese companies manufacture products here. From Canon, to Bridgestone, to Panasonic, to Sony and Toyota. And a thousand more that you have never heard of. They've got billions invested in Vietnam, and if people start walking out on them, like at the Nikkō plant, they're in trouble. The Second World War generation is pretty much all dead, but the bitterness and hatred for the Japanese has been handed down through the generations like a fine wine."

Later that night, we were able to connect with Bao, who looked worn out with dark circles under his eyes. He said the more he thought about it, his best guess was that Nachi was still in Hoi An.

"She could be anywhere, but considering that the massacre was here and they grabbed her here, our best chance is to find her here. Whoever is doing this is definitely into the symbolism of this place."

Hoi An is a small city of some one hundred and twenty thousand people. From the sixteenth century, it had been a major trading port right on the Gulf of Tonkin, with the largest harbor in Southeast Asia. The Chinese, the Dutch, the Portuguese, and the Japanese had all settled in the town to run their trading businesses.

In the eighteenth century, it had gone into a decline caused by political strife and the fact that the mouth of the Thu Bon River silted up, limiting the size of ships that could enter the harbor. It was originally a culturally divided city, with the Japanese settlement across the river connected by what is still called the "Japanese Covered Bridge." It almost looked like a New England covered bridge, except it had a Buddhist temple connected to one side of the structure that was guarded by two pairs of weathered statues of monkeys and dogs on each side.

A couple of Bao's detectives brought in a large easel. They flipped over the white top page to reveal a map of Hoi An and the surrounding area. Bao stood by the easel and said to his men in Vietnamese as Hai translated, "We must ask ourselves, who would want to kidnap this woman and threaten her with death? So far there is no money involved, so following the money will not work."

He lit up a cigarette, even though they were banned at the resort, and continued. "We must ask, who has the most to gain by acknowledging this atrocity? First, there are the Vietnamese people, who hate the Japanese for what they did here, in China, and in the Philippines.

"For them, it is not only all the murders of thousands but also the Japanese refusal to admit what they've done. To this day, the Rape of Nanking does not appear in Japanese history books that are taught to their children growing up. The Hoi An Massacre is another example of their crimes against humanity that they've covered up."

He flicked ashes from his cigarette into a coffee cup and continued. "But let us consider that this kidnapping could also come from Japan itself, and they could have additional motives.

"It is for this reason that I want us to search the Japanese district of Hoi An." Bao got very serious.

"But I want to do this as quietly as possible, with plainclothes detectives only. We will work in teams of three, with at least one officer who speaks Japanese. I want every bar, shop, and restaurant covered—every business. Talk to your Japanese contacts and snitches.

"Don't be afraid to spend money either. Bribes can be very effective given the right situation. Also tell them there may be a big reward. Who knows? There may be. Above all, show her picture around, even to the beggars on the street.

"Our basic tactic is to flood a block on all four sides as quietly as possible and work our way in. Then we go on to the next block."

It was either the best or the worst night to search the Japanese district of town. It was the night of Hoi An's monthly Lantern Festival, which had become a major tourist attraction. The city killed the streetlights, and in all restaurants and shops, radios and TVs were turned off—as well as all the neon lights. The streets, bridges, bars, and restaurants were all lit with hundreds of multicolored hanging lanterns, blowing like paper rainbows in the wind under a coal-black sky.

CHAPTER 10

Bao had a good dozen detectives assembled in a garage outside of town. When it came to street clothes, they did not fool around. Several of them were dressed as farm laborers, wearing *áo cánh* pajamas, conical straw hats, and sandals with dried mud on their feet. They did not look like cops, just some poor workers right out of a rice paddy.

Several others were dressed as drunken businessmen out celebrating a corporate victory, with their ties askew, and one guy carrying a bottle of sake.

Bao asked for quiet and said in Vietnamese, "Our strategy is to go after restaurants and bars that have takeout food. Find out if they've been delivering to unusual places or if anyone is buying a lot of food on a daily basis.

"Talk to their delivery people and the tuk tuk drivers the restaurants use to deliver. Same is true of the bars. Interview everyone who takes orders. Ask what kind of Japanese accents they have and if they are from their homeland; they could sound a lot different than our local people."

We went off into the night: Hoi An shimmered in the competing pastel colors of the lanterns. Block after block there were two-hundred-year-old buildings that had been untouched by combat. Hai and I went out with a team of detectives, who were dressed like yahoo tourists in oversized Nike T-shirts and loud Hawaiian shirts. One guy even had a sweatshirt with a picture of Godzilla on it. I wore a blue polo shirt and jeans.

They'd go into a place, hang around for a while, and then get the manager off in a corner, where they would tell him who they were and what they wanted. Some gave blank stares or were scared, but others were helpful. The detectives would then talk to their order-takers and delivery guys—showing Nachi's picture and always asking if they'd seen anything unusual or suspicious.

This went on for hours as we went from place to place. A feeling of futility started to set in. At least it did with me because finding anything at midnight in the dark was clearly a long shot.

We ended up going to a newer café called Sushi Sushi, which was housed in an old French police station. After talking to the manager and his people who took food orders, the detectives waited around for the café's delivery guy to return. After a half hour, he rolled up to the restaurant on a motorbike with a big wire basket mounted to the front. He was a little fellow, maybe four feet eleven. When they asked if he'd seen anything out of the ordinary, he brightened up and started speaking rapid Vietnamese.

Hai translated, "He is saying he'd been making deliveries to a warehouse down by the river where nobody lives. He said it was always the same Japanese guy at the door who paid for their food and that sometimes the same guy would come to Sushi Sushi to pick up orders himself."

For such an old building, the café had an excellent security-camera system. We followed the manager into a room behind the bar and began reviewing the last five days of footage from a camera mounted over the cash register. It was ponderous going through hours of digital images, speeding up and slowing down so that the delivery man could study the customers' faces.

Thirty minutes into it, he pointed to the screen and said, "That's the guy." He was a young man in his twenties with hooded eyes and round, black-framed glasses. His image remained motionless on the screen.

After that, one of the detectives got Bao on the phone and organized a team to go check out the warehouse. He was only a few blocks away, so in minutes they had a total of ten guys on scooters, some of them in uniform. Hai and I got rides with them. Hai took the GoPro off his chest mount, switched the program to low light, and continued shooting as he rode on the back of the scooter, holding the camera with his good hand.

There was a long pier next to the warehouse. We spoke in whispers. The building was entirely blacked out. The detectives had brought the delivery guy along so that they could be certain of the location.

They convinced him to walk up the steel steps to the warehouse door and ring the bell. After a minute, a light went on over the door. It came open about a foot, but the man with the round, black-framed glasses slammed it shut when he saw us. Two of the detectives went up and started pounding on the door and yelling in Vietnamese. It was then that we heard the burble of an outboard engine starting, right under the building.

We ran to the end of the pier and saw a black ski boat with a glowing center console slowly motoring out from under the warehouse. There were two men and what looked like a woman with a hood over her head. The cops yelled down for them to stop.

As the boat neared the center of the river, it turned upstream, and the driver gave the boat's two big outboards full power. And then they were gone—the black boat, the black river, and a town that liked to shut the lights off on certain nights.

CHAPTER *11*

ao put a call in for a police boat, but it was a long time before they came. It might have been ten minutes, but it felt like a year. Bao yelled down from the pier and gave instructions to the three officers on the patrol craft. He described the black ski boat and told them to search the river until they found it.

A little over an hour later, they discovered it tied up to a small floating pier about five miles upstream. They sent the patrol boat back for us, and we went up the dark river with the boat's searchlight leading the way.

The black boat rocked as our wake hit it. There was already an evidence team on board, carrying big flashlights, inspecting the boat. Each of them wore white latex gloves, and they were shooting every inch with a camera. One of the team members was able to hot-wire the ignition under the console and get the engines to fire up, turning on the navigation system, which had a GPS display with a touch screen.

He fiddled with the contrast and brightness until they could plainly see clear fingerprints standing out from the touch screen buttons. They took digital micropictures of every print and e-mailed them to both the Japanese and Vietnamese national criminal databases.

It was after two in the morning, and I was in a land beyond tiredness. The boat rocked as the men worked. Finally they took mercy on us and the police took us back down the river, followed by a squad car ride back to The Nam Hai.

I barely took my shoes off as I passed out on the bed with my clothes on. I fell asleep and went into an unstoppable dream.

We were attacking a bridge, and the NVA soldiers were firing from every building on the other side of the Perfume River. The commander said that his tanks were too heavy for the bridge, so they lined them up on the shore and started shelling the other side.

The Army of the Republic of South Vietnam (ARVN) had lighter tanks, but they refused an order to attack. So it ended up with our guys attacking the bridge on foot. There was a machine gun that was knocking down guys before they even got halfway. But there was one marine who kept on running across the bridge, throwing two grenades that blew up the machine-gun crew. I saw this from across the river next to the tanks. Then we were next. I felt a wave of nausea and threw up as we ran toward the bridge.

We ran across under heavy fire. Every second I was certain I was going to get hit, the rounds bouncing off the steel structure. We were able to get two platoons across, but then the roof caved in. We went left and immediately came under a brutal shower of small-arms and recoilless-rifle fire from the Citadel wall. With the pounding that we were taking, we were forced to withdraw back across the bridge, taking even more casualties.

The whole time we're fighting, parts of Psalm 23 kept repeating in my head:

> *"The Lord is my shepherd.*

> *Yea, though I walk through the valley of the*

shadow of death, I will fear no evil:
for thou art with me;
thy rod and thy staff they comfort me.

Thou preparest a table before me
in the presence of mine enemies:
thou anointest my head with oil;
my cup runneth over.

Surely goodness and mercy
shall follow me all the days of my life:
and I will dwell in the house
of the Lord forever."

I kept repeating it, fighting to keep my terror at bay.

I'd heard it when the chaplain would give last rights, even though the chaplain was wounded pretty badly himself. I saw a couple of our guys carry the chaplain over and put him beside a marine who was hopelessly wounded and about to die. Through the gunfire and explosions, I could hear his calm fatherly voice: "The Lord is my shepherd."

We were in a pitched battle that seemed like it would go on until everyone was dead. Even in the midst of total chaos, I was amazed at what a seventeen-year-old, right out of high school, could do. There were three of these kids up on the second story of a building with a pitched tile roof. The roof had moss on the tile, and the pitch was steep. They had a bazooka, which they were using to blow up a building one block over. They would load the bazooka below the roofline and then pop up and fire before the NVA could fire back.

Another shaped-charge rocket would be crawled up the roof by a marine. They then would change their position, reload, pop up, and let them have it.

I also saw a marine walk into fire when he couldn't take it anymore.

CHAPTER *12*

I awoke feeling bewildered—shaking and sweating even though the air conditioning was on high. I called Tao and ordered breakfast, turned on the Keurig and the big-screen TV. Immediately, there was a BBC report from Hanoi in front of the Nikkō factory.

It had been filmed during the night while there were an estimated ten thousand employees standing in the parking lot next to the plant. They were chanting, "No more lies," in Vietnamese. There were two rows of several hundred cops in black riot gear guarding the factory.

The cops stood shoulder to shoulder in front of the entrance to the plant. Even though it was the third day of the walkout, the crowd of employees still showed great energy. "No more lies." There were thousands of flashing cell-phones lights.

The British reporter pointed out that this was a highly unusual situation, as the Japanese plant supervisors had walked out themselves to show solidarity with their Vietnamese workers. A huge Jumbotron, with a semitrailer-mounted video screen, was parked to the right of the main entrance. Even more remarkable, the chairman of Nikkō, Shiro Kobayashi, came on the screen. A distinguished, older Japanese gentleman, he spoke slowly in English with a Vietnamese translation in large letters on the bottom of the HD picture.

"Today we reach out to our most valued Vietnamese colleagues, with great sorrow for the slaughter of innocent Vietnamese by Japanese forces many years ago. I have made it my mission to appeal to our Japanese prime minister to end the deception and cruel lies that have been too long a part of our culture.

"Now, our government says that they will 'never negotiate with kidnappers,' but it is really a policy of keeping the truth hidden from the world and our Japanese citizens themselves. Especially now that they would let another person die, an innocent woman, to cover our shame while they poison our relationship with our Vietnamese friends.

"If our government does not respond honestly to the demands for the truth about Hoi An by the deadline, the prime minister and his cabinet will be removed from office. Because the no confidence votes in the Diet, our parliament, I am certain, will be there. And a new government will be formed."

With that, the red Vietnamese flag with its gold star in the center came on the screen, waving in the breeze, as they played the Vietnamese national anthem— "Song of Marching Troops." With a chorus of soldiers singing, the English translation appeared at the bottom of the screen:

Soldiers of Vietnam, we go forward.

The gold star of our flag in the wind.

Leading our people, our native land,

Out of misery and suffering.

Let us join our efforts in the fight

For the building of a new life.

Let us stand up and break our chains.

For too long we have swallowed our hatred.

Let us keep ready for all sacrifices,

And our life will be radiant.

Ceaselessly for the people's cause we struggle,

Hastening to the battlefield! Forward!

All together advancing!

For one eternal Vietnam.

The immense crowd of people sang along. The BBC broadcasted the complete event. Later there were television reports of massive worker walkouts at a Fuji Xerox photocopier factory and at Panasonic Digital.

I called Hai, and he came over with his laptop. He had seen the BBC report from the Nikkō plant. He told me that the Nikkō chairman is a very respected man in Vietnam and that the speech had gone instantly viral on Twitter, Facebook, and Instagram, and there'd been almost a million YouTube hits from Japan, Vietnam, and many parts of the world. And that was just in a few hours.

Down at the conference center, there were dozens of cops who'd been up all night searching the warehouse and all around the floating pier where they'd found the boat. They looked fried, red eyed, grim. Some slept on cots that The Nam Hai staff had brought in, and there was a cook who worked out of a hospitality kitchen down the hall—all financed by Oshima's *blank check*.

Bao and two of his detectives were looking at the big map of Hoi An, trying to figure out where to search next. They'd come up empty searching the area around the boat. Divers had done a grid search, only to find rusting lawn furniture and an endless number of crushed beer cans. But then a detective, who was seated at the big conference table, called Bao over to look at his laptop.

The detective said in rapid Vietnamese, "We have a match for one of the prints we got off the nav screen. The guy is Japanese. He's here on a student visa. His name is Hideki Koji. He's been arrested twice for fighting with police during student protests in Tokyo. He was charged with throwing a tear-gas canister back at the police after the police had thrown it at them. The charges were eventually dropped, but they got his fingerprints. He's supposed to be a student at Da Nang University of Technology."

CHAPTER *13*

D a Nang was a short drive from Hoi An, especially going one hundred miles per hour, along with a pack of Hoi An police squad cars. They had an address for a student dormitory at the university. After a bit of driving around, they found the dorm—a four-story, glass-walled building. There were only a few people on the first floor. The detectives weren't just looking for his room; they were looking for Hideki Koji and anyone who knew him. No search warrants, no Miranda rights. They just went around bracing the college kids like they'd committed a crime.

"Did you know him?"

"How well?"

"When was the last time you saw him?"

"Who were his friends?"

"His girlfriend?

"What was he studying?"

"Who were his Japanese friends?"

"His Vietnamese friends?"

"Was there anything unusual about him?"

"You know that lying to the police is a crime?"

They weren't "good cop, bad cop." They were just furious bad cops. The college kids cowered, and the cops yelled at them for not speaking louder. They assembled all the kids from the dorm in the dining room. Then in came tough guy Bao, and he was the good cop.

"I appeal to you, as citizens and as visitors to Vietnam, to help us in the investigation of the abduction of Nachi Tanaka. I know you are innocent students, but any small bit of information you could give us will be greatly appreciated and could possibly save a woman's life. To that end, we would like to interview each of you, individually."

The detectives searched Hideki Koji's room and

found a cell phone taped to the underside of his desk. Trying not to disturb any fingerprints, they took a good ten minutes getting the phone peeled off and then dropped it into a plastic bag. It was a new silver iPhone 6s with fingerprint encryption.

Hai asked a detective, "How are you going to get into his phone?"

"Are you kidding?" the detective said. "We've got his fingerprints from the boat."

The interrogation of the students went on for hours. Each one was grilled by two-man teams. There were nearly forty students, and most of them had never heard of Hideki Koji. But there was one person who knew a lot: his roommate and friend, Kei Ichiro.

He could speak Vietnamese. The detectives let the other kids go and gave Kei their full attention. He said he was twenty years old and had gone to school with Hideki in Japan, and they had come to Da Nang to study civil engineering. "We were both sponsored by Takahashi Corporation, a Japanese construction company, which was doing large road-construction projects around Hanoi, like the new superhighway going to Ha Long Bay."

After getting their degrees, they were committed to working for the company for five years. He claimed that Hideki was a serious student and that all he focused on was knowing everything about bridge construction—all the options.

Kei brushed back his long black hair and said, "Hideki was in some student demonstrations in Tokyo about nuclear power after the earthquake, tsunami, and meltdown of the Fukushima Daiichi Nuclear Power Plant."

He looked up at us and said, "More than eighty percent of the Japanese say they are antinuclear and distrust government information on radiation.

"There was a big 2011 investigation that revealed a long history of Japanese nuclear-power companies conspiring with the government to manipulate public opinion in their favor. Hideki hated this. He would go on and on about how we were pawns while so many lives are at stake. He refused to be taken in by them.

"When they restarted the Oi Nuclear Power Plant, he was very angry. He would say, 'We are like sheep, and they are traitors to our people.'"

The detectives showed him the plastic bag with the

cell phone that had been hidden under Hideki's desk. He said he'd never seen it or knew anything about it. He seemed sincere and honest.

"Hideki's phone was black and made by Samsung, not Apple."

No one in the dorm had seen him for a week. The detectives took the hidden phone and his laptop, and we went in convoy back to The Nam Hai.

CHAPTER 14

The big conference room had been cleaned up and smelled of a strong disinfectant air freshener. The TV was tuned to CCTV, China Central Television. The report covered a big demonstration going on in Beijing, in front of the Japanese Embassy. The report said, "Events in Vietnam have now set off the people's hatred for the Japanese, who murdered millions of Chinese in the Second Word War."

The report, which was subtitled in English, cited the 1937 Nanking Massacre, where an estimated twenty thousand women were raped and murdered and where hundreds of thousands of Chinese civilians and disarmed soldiers were killed. The Japanese military records of the killings were deliberately kept secret or destroyed, but the International Military Tribunal of the Far East estimated that over 300,000 Chinese were killed in a six-week orgy of violence. And then the Chinese report went right to present day, when the current Japanese prime minister had personally visited the Yasukuni Shrine. There enshrined in a place of honor are 1,618 convicted Japanese war criminals, including fourteen "Class A" mass murderers.

It was like the Japanese enjoyed baiting the Chinese and the Vietnamese. The prime minister had brought a large bouquet of flowers to the Yasukuni Shrine. So there was now a state-sponsored riot in front of the Japanese Embassy in Beijing, as the shutdown of Japanese businesses and factories in Vietnam continued airing on the local news channels.

The scene of the demonstration was interrupted by a "Special Report" from Kyoto, Japan. There on the screen sat an older, elegant woman named Ruri Tanaka. She was Nachi's widowed mother. She sat on a leather couch in a small living room with a white rug, a coffee table, and green flower-print walls. She wore a tan shirtwaist dress and looked remarkably like Nachi, except she had delicate crow's-feet around her eyes.

Speaking in Japanese, "I think they took my daughter because she discovered the story. It has always been our family's secret that my father-in-law, Akio Tanaka, had executed many innocent people during the Pacific War. It is our family shame. And now they are going to kill her for it."

The picture returned to the Japanese reporter who recounted the story of Nachi's abduction, the Japanese government's silence, the uproar in Vietnam and China, and Nachi's threatened execution in three days—seventy-two hours.

Bao's men had been attacking Hideki's laptop and iPhone. They were able to transfer a copy of his thumbprint to the phone's encryption screen. It flashed twice, and they were in—no password needed. They went through the phone's history, trying to match up numbers from The Nam Hai people: the hotel operator, the hotel driver, Tao the butler, and the golf cart driver, who took her back to her room before she was driven to Hoi An.

They had two detectives, one who spoke credible Japanese, start tracing all the other numbers against a database of cell phone users. They even went so far as to blind call and say, "Hideki told me to call you. He's in trouble and needs your help." The plan was that if they got a person to respond, they would ask to meet them at a restaurant in Hoi An that they had staked out.

In most five-star hotels, room phones come with a directory of numbers you can call for various services, from a room-service meal to spa treatments. But not at The Nam Hai. There, each phone had a small sign that read "Dial zero, and we'll take care of everything." So when you punched that one number, you were immediately connected to your personal butler, or his backup, and the butler would take care of anything that you could possibly want.

Romantic torchlight dinner on the beach? They ask, "What time would you like it?" A limo to go to Da Nang? They ask, "Is an S-Class Mercedes okay?" Tour guides, cooking lessons, sailing trips, in-room massages, special wines, a vast selection of movies, robes, towels, helicopter rides, a business assistant, laundry, dry cleaners—if you could think it up, they would get it for you. The butler also took phone messages for you. But still I was shocked when they found Tao's cell phone number in Hideki's phone. Bao nodded his head and said to the seven cops sitting at the table, "Let's go talk to this kid."

CHAPTER *15*

They didn't have to go far. Our compound was a couple hundred yards away. Of course, for once he wasn't there. His backup met us and said it was Tao's night off. He had no idea where he'd gone, but he thought Tao should be back by midnight. There was nothing to do but wait.

It was a quiet night. The water gurgled in the koi pond. The orange fish flashed through the underwater lights, occasionally breaking the surface to go after a bug. The compound's outdoor sound system filled the evening with Zen Buddhist meditation music. It was spare, haunting, and mystical, like walking through the jungle at night with all the creatures making strange musical sounds.

After an hour, Tao came through the front gate,

riding an old-fashioned balloon-tire bike. Bao introduced himself and asked him to come into the living room in the big main house.

"We have your cell phone records," Bao said. "We want to ask you about several calls that were made to you. I want you to think back clearly and accurately. On the day Nachi was abducted, you took a call at 2:19 p.m. Could you tell us who it was from?"

Bao pulled out Tao's phone and showed him the number on the list of recent calls.

Tao stared at the number for a moment, "It was a man from Oshima Advertising in Tokyo. He asked for Nachi. I told him she was out with a shooting crew."

"Did he give you his name?" Bao asked.

"No, he just said he would call back later."

"There is a record of another call at 4:39 p.m. Do you remember that?" Bao continued.

"Yes, it was the agency again, and I told him she was still out with the crew."

Bao then asked about a call at 10:40 p.m.

Tao confirmed, "It was the same man from the

agency. I told him she'd gone to Hoi An to find a drugstore, but she would be back soon. He never called back, and she never came back."

Bao said, "The person you talked to was in Hoi An, not Tokyo. We think he was one of the people who abducted her. You're free to go, but under no circumstances are you to talk to anyone about what you have told us."

I believed Tao. The guys who abducted her knew exactly where she was at the resort.

This was not the first job I had done for Oshima. In fact, it was my fifth big project with an Oshima subsidiary—Oshima Creative Force, which operated on its own within the huge agency. Oshima had a mighty fifty-two-story office tower in Tokyo, which barely housed a fraction of the company's worldwide operations. They were by far the most powerful agency in Japan, and the company was run much differently than an American ad agency.

In the States, typically, a company would call an agency review, where six to ten prospective agencies would present their advertising and creative ideas to the company's marketing managers. It was winner take all.

One agency would be selected to do the advertising—sometimes social media and public relations, too.

But with Oshima, they demanded much more control of the process. They insisted on controlling the company's marketing decisions from top to bottom. So the company's marketing department ended up answering to Oshima. If you didn't like it, they wouldn't work for you. Doing it their way, they'd been wildly successful at turning companies around, although their methods, with things like mass firings and radical changes in strategy, were considered draconian.

I had gone to the Oshima offices several times for meetings with the British creative team that focused on luxury-travel accounts. They had seen a commercial I'd done for Cathay Pacific Airways, named "The Flight of Your Dreams." It won a first-place Clio Award, and that became my ticket to do a campaign for the Peninsula Hotel in Hong Kong—the city's most legendary five-star property. One month of shooting and editing had resulted in a short movie for the web, as well as individual TV commercials. It was my first job with Nachi.

The creative people were terrific to work with. They'd have basic storyboards, but after that, they let us run wild. We did dramatic helicopter shots at night with the Peninsula lit up with searchlights glowing across Hong Kong's Victoria Harbour.

We staged a camera crane shot of high tea in the hotel's posh lobby. It started with a shot of a small orchestra playing the Brandenburg Concerto on the second-story balcony. The camera then swept down and followed a waiter from above, bringing a tall tray of pastries, fresh scones and finger sandwiches to an elegant Asian couple seated across the room. There were sixty extras seated at the other tables, all dressed to the nines.

We also layered in a historical narrative of the hotel as the "Grand Dame of the Far East," including the hotel's gigantic fleet of brand-new Peninsula-green Rolls-Royces and recounted all the famous figures who called the Peninsula home, from Winston Churchill to Morgan Freeman.

After that, the team at Oshima asked me to do the Vietnam project, and I had really wondered if I could or should do it. I had sworn I'd never go back.

Ever since the war, I had made it my mission to stay away from the sadness and the ghostly memories of all the people who had been lost—all for nothing. I remembered Defense Secretary Robert McNamara's tearful apology years later and the pain of knowing that even though we had the best of intentions, we had been totally wrong and, in the process, ended up killing several million Vietnamese.

McNamara was the absolute architect of the war; he had presided over the loss of more than fifty thousand Americans, leaving hundreds of thousands of men fucked up for life.

He came away saying, "The American failure in Vietnam was seeing the enemy through the prism of the Cold War, as a domino that would topple the nations of Asia if it succeeded."

He had thought it was the march of communism, when the fact was that the majority of Vietnamese hated the Chinese, and it was really a civil war, North versus South, like the bloody Civil War we'd had in our own country.

I loved shooting commercials because it was upbeat, fresh, audacious, and no one got killed. Going back to Vietnam was going back to the sadness I had avoided for a long time.

I'd look into the eyes of these sweet, kind people and try to fathom the fact that we had wanted to kill them in big numbers for wanting to rule their own country. An old waiter in Le Beaulieu, the French restaurant at the Metropole, told me how bad it had been for them. He had been a teenaged NVA soldier on a troop train going south at night—the train was totally blacked out.

"But the B-52s caught up with us and took out the entire train with a gigantic string of bombs. In five seconds, twenty thousand men were dead," he said in halting English.

He told of being machine-gunned by Cobra attack helicopters, where an entire company was wiped out. "I was the only one in my company to come back. We paid a big price."

Deep in my heart, I knew exactly what he was talking about. We shook hands as I looked into his old yellowing eyes.

CHAPTER *16*

The room was dark as I sat up in my bed and looked out at the landscape lighting that lit up the palm trees and the pool. I wanted to run away from the sadness like it was a physical presence—block it all out—but all I could think about was one afternoon in Hue when we'd been in the midst of a fierce firefight. We were firing from a drainage ditch along a fence line. With us was a young mother carrying an infant, along with five other little kids. They were so scared. We were so scared. The kids were terrified and crying. The young mother was beautiful, dignified, hugging the infant in the drainage ditch, her hand cradling its head as we laid down fire and kept on attacking.

I never saw them again—but they have stayed with me forever.

The phone rang. It was Hai, "The Japanese prime minister's office has issued a blanket denial. They sent out a press secretary who read a statement saying that the story of the Hoi An Massacre was a total fabrication created by dark political forces intent on bringing down the prime minister and his government. Further, they repeated they had no record of the massacre or of Colonel Akio Tanaka having any part in the event. He went on to say, 'It has always been our unshakable policy to never negotiate with kidnappers, no matter what their demands, especially when this story is not true and dishonors the memory of our war dead.'"

Hai said he'd come over in a couple of minutes. I turned on a few of the house lights and made a cup of coffee. Hai walked in carrying his laptop.

"You've got to see this," he exclaimed. "The prime minister of Japan has a Facebook page."

"What?"

"I know. Maybe every leader does, but you've got to see this thing he posted today."

Hai flipped around the laptop, and there was a picture of the prime minister bowing deeply in front of a large flower display in the shape of Mount Fuji.

On the right was a heading that read, "A message from our prime minister," followed by his words: "Today I visited Chidorigafuchi National Cemetery to pay my respects and conducted a memorial ceremony for the war dead. There, before the souls who died, I silently joined my hands in prayer and bowed my head to pray for their repose. At the same time, I pledged to these souls that Japan will continue into the future to follow a never-changing path toward peace.

"With my eyes fixed firmly ahead, I want to carve out the future of this country for the sake of the generation who is alive at this moment and for the generations of tomorrow, as we engrave into our hearts the precious lessons left by our ancestors."

I could not believe that he'd said it, that he'd done it, at exactly this time. But because it was Facebook, there were hundreds of comments below his statement. The first one said, "The blood of the Vietnamese is covering you. Their cries will disturb your sleep. These murders will shorten your life, and the destruction of their families will destroy yours."

CHAPTER *17*

Hai asserted, "The way he is stonewalling this is not going to work if they kill Nachi. He knows what's going on. He thinks if he admits to Hoi An that he will dishonor their war dead—for being the bunch of murderous thugs they were, instead of revered ancestors. He's trying to tough it out, but I don't think it's going to work this time."

"Why not?" I asked.

"Because his conservative Liberal Democratic Party and the New Komeito Party have a coalition that is totally in bed with the big corporations, and the corporations are mad as hell.

"The chairman of Nikkō," Hai continued, pointing at a newsfeed, "went on the Nippon News Network last night and said that the prime minister's arrogance was destroying relationships built over many years with our Vietnamese and Chinese partners and that he was destroying Japanese jobs and our reputation as fair and honest people.

"The chairman said, 'This is not saving face; this is lying about the truth.'"

Hai looked up at me from his iPhone. He had set a timer to when Nachi was supposed to be executed. He held it up so that I could see the minutes ticking down: "49 hours and 34 minutes" and then "49:33, 49:32, 49:31…"

I wanted to pretend that it was not really happening, that it was all a bad dream, and that we'd all be on a happy advertising shoot in the morning with a gorgeous girl telling us where we'd be going that day. She'd hand out a shot list that made you tired just looking at it, especially with the heat and humidity.

But after that first shot of the day, everything would come alive with an energy that would last until midnight. Like the camera car flying down a beautiful boulevard in Ho Chi Minh City, when Nachi paid off ten policemen to stop the traffic in both directions while we did the shot twice, in less than ten minutes.

But, of course, this was not the case. I wanted to believe that they wouldn't kill Nachi and that somehow she'd be found. Still, I could feel the rage building inside me.

Hai and I took a walk down the beach, heading for the reception center that connected to a beautiful Western-themed restaurant and bar. The resort sparkled with a ribbon of thousands of white lights set beside the black of the ocean. We sat at the bar and ordered real drinks—gin and tonics made with Hendrick's Gin and a big lime—along with Hai's request to "go easy on the tonic."

Hai's full name was Bach Tuyên Hai. He was the most overeducated tour guide, translator, and production assistant I'd ever met. He had a master's degree and PhD in economics, and taught courses at Vietnam National University in Hanoi. He was about five feet six inches tall, with a slicked-back Elvis pompadour that made him look like he was five feet ten.

"Teaching doesn't pay very much," he revealed, "so I have a real-estate management company in Hanoi, as well as the tours. It's a nice life. I have a two-year-old son and a lovely wife, Lan, who works with me."

He pulled up pictures on his phone of his young wife and son, and of a ninety-year-old grandmother who lived with them, along with a dog named Lucky. They lived in a handsome house, which was one block away from Hanoi's West Lake. It was a four-story, yellow-stucco building with Juliet balconies, green shutters, and an impressive view of Hanoi's largest lake from the upper floors—like another land, far away.

CHAPTER *18*

After we finished our drinks, we walked down a lighted path to the conference center. Five tired-looking detectives sat around the table, working on their computers or talking on phones in quiet voices. One of the detectives told us they had one lead west of town, where a witness at an intersection had seen a tan Nissan minivan go by with someone that looked like Nachi.

It was a pretty thin lead without a license-plate number, but they had sent out a bunch of cops on scooters to look for a tan Nissan minivan.

Bao and one of his men came into the room. Loosening his tie as he walked around the table, he said, "They put out a notice on YouTube that Nachi will be giving her final message in thirty minutes."

"Final message? What does that mean?" I interrupted.

"That's what it said, in English, Japanese, and Vietnamese. There was no picture of her, just white type on a black screen."

Hai held up the countdown clock on his iPhone. It now displayed "36:10"—thirty-six hours, ten minutes. One of the detectives got the YouTube announcement on his computer. It was just like Bao had said—plain type in three languages.

The AV people from the resort wheeled in a large flat-screen TV and hooked it up to a computer and the Internet. The room started to fill up with staff from the resort and more cops. A Tokyo news crew was pleading with Bao to let them film the room when Nachi came on. They promised to work as a pool camera and feed their footage to the other networks.

I walked outside, checking my watch every couple of minutes. Everything seemed to be slowing down— even the sound of the surf breaking on the shore. I went back in and sat next to Hai. The room had a muffled murmur to it as it filled with cops, hotel staff, and two camera crews. I sat back in my chair and breathed deeply, trying to calm myself.

The YouTube page with Nachi's other videos came up on the big screen. A half hour came and went, with nothing new coming up. But then a rectangular picture of Nachi's face appeared next to the other videos from the abduction. A cursor arrow popped up on the screen and clicked on Nachi's face.

There was an audible gasp in the room when she came into view. Nachi's head was shaved, and she was wearing a wrinkled white t-shirt. She sat outside, roped to a chair in front of a small Vietnamese farmhouse with a thatched roof. I felt sick; the acid was coming up in my throat. By the look of things, they were using car headlights to illuminate the scene.

"I am Nachi Tanaka; I was raised in Japan as a Buddhist and a Christian. There is a passage in the Bible that says, 'The sins of the fathers shall be visited on sons from generation to generation.' In my case, it is not a son but a daughter. In less than thirty-four hours, I will be burned to death, exactly as so many Vietnamese were burned to death in Hoi An." Her voice broke at the end.

"The only thing that can stop this from happening

is the will of the Japanese government to make things right with the Vietnamese people, starting with the truth." Tearing up, she continued. "Mother and Kiki, I want to tell you I love you so much. I am filled with sadness and shame that this is our family story. Please be strong for me. I will always be with you."

Hai had tears in his eyes. So did I, as did all of these other people I had never seen before: chambermaids, waiters, bartenders, groundskeepers, and lots of cops. Silently we filed out of the room into the night air.

She had looked beaten. Worst of all, it was clear from the fear in her eyes that she knew what was going to happen. They were going to kill her in less than thirty-four hours.

I wished I'd never come back.

CHAPTER 19

We walked back to the compound and started watching the overnight news channels from Japan. We kept switching back and forth from the Fuji News Network to NHK World to the Nippon News Network. We watched a stand-up news report from in front of the Japanese prime minister's new residence, which had been custom built for him.

The reporter recounted the story that the prime minister had refused to live in the original building that had been completed in 1929—because of ghosts. One prime minister had been assassinated there in 1932, and four years later there was an attempted coup by a faction from the Imperial Japanese Army. There were still bullet holes in the walls. Over the years, several former first ladies also refused to move in for fear it was haunted. There had been frequent reported sightings of men in military uniforms showing up in a nearby garden and then disappearing.

The prime minister had reportedly joked with executives from the LDG Corporation, "I don't like the idea of living here because there are ghosts. I think it could get a little crowded." He continued living in his suburban house until the new residence was built.

The reporter continued. "For the prime minister tonight, the ghosts of the past are present again: the ghosts of the Hoi An Massacre. This afternoon members of the New Komeito Party announced the end of their alliance with the prime minister's Liberal Democratic Party. All afternoon the halls of the Diet were filled with talk of a possible no-confidence vote to be taken tomorrow. At the same time, it has also been reported that the prime minister's approval rating among Japanese citizens has reached an all-time low. Just thirty-nine percent of the people polled approve of the job he is doing."

Later on another Japanese-English-speaking channel, they reported that the prime minister would address both houses of the Diet at ten the next morning. Hai said, "I can't take it anymore. I'm going to bed."

I dug around in the minibar and found a cold bottle of pinot grigio and noticed my hands were shaking. I got it uncorked and took a long drink directly from the bottle. I felt sadness, fear, rage. I could not shake the image of Nachi with her head shaved and the bewildered terror in her eyes.

I didn't want to go to sleep, but I was dead tired. I closed my eyes and tried to stop my obsessive thoughts that they were going to kill Nachi and that there was nothing we could do about it. It was all up to the goddamned prime minister, and he was denying everything.

CHAPTER *20*

Between my nightmares and the crushing reality of the situation, horrible memories kept coming up—specifically my last day of house fighting in Hue.

We were kicking in doors, sometimes using a heavy battering ram, and then tossing in grenades or a satchel charge. But the toughest job was being the first man through the door. That day I was the first man in. An NVA guy opened up with an AK-47 at very close range as I fired at him. We both went down. He looked about fifteen. Innocents killing innocents. I was hit in the shoulder and the thigh, and I could see I was bleeding out fast. I used my good hand to try to grab my femoral artery, where it was pumping out from my leg wound. I couldn't find it. I was covered in blood. I was pretty sure it was all over. "The Lord is my shepherd." But it was the two marines coming in behind me that killed the two other NVA soldiers in the house and then put a tourniquet on my leg and strapped up my shoulder.

Then there were some Huey chopper pilots who took some ridiculous chances, flying into a hot landing zone in a city park with bullets pinging off the rotors, to pick me up with two other guys who looked dead. When we took off, a big explosion blew off the door on the left side, and the Huey dropped toward the ground, but the pilots caught it and pulled up, just clearing the tree line.

I drifted in and out of consciousness. It felt like just a few minutes had passed before we were landing at an artillery firebase, which was finally shelling Hue's Citadel with huge, deafening, 155mm howitzers. I was brought into a field-hospital operating room, where I was immediately given a shot of something, and everything went black.

I woke up and tried to shake off the memory. My room at The Nam Hai was silent. I lay there a while, then finally fell back into a dreamless sleep.

CHAPTER *21*

aking up later that morning, I knew the whole thing was soon going to be decided. Tao silently brought in breakfast, arranged it on the table, and just as soundlessly disappeared. I turned on the TV with the sound off. It showed a Japanese reporter, again, doing a stand-up report in front of Japan's parliament—the Diet in Tokyo.

Hai walked in, his arm still in a sling, his Elvis pompadour moussed into place and claimed, "The prime minister is going to deny it until the end. He's barely got the votes to hang on, but if he admits to all the lies, he's definitely dead on arrival."

I still hoped for something better, but I thought he was probably right. I opened one of the big sliding doors, and the room was filled with the sound of the surf and the noise from a pack of sparrows squabbling over food under a palm tree.

We sat watching the report without talking. "I've got to go for a workout. I'll go crazy if I just sit here anymore," I told Hai.

Given the situation, The Nam Hai's spa and fitness center seemed like a totally surreal environment. Meditation music drifted through the building, as did the smell of jasmine flowers and the childlike voices of the young Vietnamese girls dressed in their matching white silk *áo dàis*, directing guests to their treadmills. I couldn't run with my titanium knee, but I got off to a fast walk. By the time I left the treadmill, it was almost eight thirty. Over at the conference center, there were more TV trucks than ever, with dozens of satellite dishes pointing straight up in the air. The Nam Hai had opened up the big ballroom, which was rapidly filling up. There was a large television on the stage that was tuned to the Nippon News Network. It was 9:35 a.m.

Everyone waited quietly. Then at precisely ten o'clock, a picture of the combined session of the Diet of Japan came on the big screen. The cameras panned the massive mahogany-lined chamber, where every seat was taken. The prime minister walked up the carpeted steps and stumbled, quickly grabbing the railing and steadying himself as he continued to the podium.

He began by saying, "Today I come to you with a deep sense of outrage at the complete and utter lies that are being put at the feet of the soldiers who so valiantly defended our country during the Pacific War. These men fought and died in the most honorable tradition of the Imperial Japanese Army. But now there are depraved forces hiding in the shadows, who have fabricated a story of a massacre in Indochina that never involved our forces.

"On its most basic level, this is clearly a conspiracy to discredit our government and dishonor the memory of those who gave everything to safeguard our homeland. We will not give into blackmail, ever. We will not admit culpability in crimes that are a diabolical work of complete fiction."

It was done. The prime minister wasn't backing down. Nachi was going to die.

CHAPTER 22

Clapping began on the right side of the chamber, but nowhere else. The majority of the Diet was seated and silent. The prime minister left the podium.

The picture cut away to an English-speaking reporter standing outside in front of the Diet. He said, "It's as if thousands of people appeared out of nowhere. There have been several reports that this is a flash mob created by social-media connections."

The camera swept the crowd where a one-hundred-foot red banner was unrolled. Large white Japanese letters began to form the message "Let Us Now Face the Shame of Our Past," and one that read, "The Lies Must End." The reporter pointed out a hand-lettered sign that read, "There is no honor in murdering the innocent."

With that, hundreds of Japanese riot police with shields and batons entered the scene from a side street, followed by armored trucks with water cannons. The police wore black helmets and bulletproof vests. Thousands of demonstrators wearing white helmets charged the police with wooden telephone poles; hundreds of people ran with the poles directly into the police lines, like some medieval movie.

The water cannons started firing; tear gas hit the demonstrators with large plumes of gray smoke. The crowd started throwing Molotov cocktails at the police vehicles. Several hit the roof of a water cannon with big bursts of flames, which were promptly put out by another water cannon next to it.

"This is unbelievable," Hai said. "This is Japan. I never thought the Japanese would go to battle for us."

The two sides surged back and forth. The riot police had on black gas masks, so it looked like hundreds of Darth Vaders were taking on thousands of kids wearing white crash helmets, many with gas masks and facemasks themselves.

The ballroom started vibrating with the "whop, whop, whop" of a helicopter coming low over the building. We went outside and saw a Russian-made Vietnamese military helicopter land in an empty parking lot near the stonewalled entrance to The Nam Hai. It was as big as a city bus—unbelievably evil looking and loud. It was bright yellow, a red Vietnamese flag with its gold star was painted over the side door behind the pilots. The engines powered down, and Bao and a couple of his men walked out to meet the pilots, carrying rolled-up maps, computers, satellite phones, and a suitcase.

When we walked up, Bao already had a map spread out on a fold-down table in the middle of a helicopter cabin that could seat twenty people. I had no idea what they were saying, but could see that Bao was pointing to an area west of Hoi An. I also heard the word "Nissan" go by in a flurry of Vietnamese.

As we buckled our seat belts, Hai told me that they were still looking out in the countryside for a tan Nissan minivan that had been sighted a second time at a gas station near where the massacres took place. There had been a bald-headed woman in the back seat.

The big turbines on the helicopter started powering up; the giant blades rotated slowly, coming up to speed, taking off with a guttural roar. We flew west into the countryside. With us were six other Hoi An police officers dressed in military gear, with two German shepherds. One of the cops opened the suitcase, which was filled with Nachi's clothes. He rubbed the dogs' noses with a sweater, a jacket, and her underwear. The dogs focused on the suitcase, memorizing her scent.

CHAPTER 23

Bao had satellite photos of different farmhouses that looked like the one where Nachi had been tied up. The photos were all looking straight down, so all I could tell was that they had thatched roofs. I thought about the images of Nachi on YouTube, wondering if the farmhouse we were approaching was the place.

We came in for a landing on a rice-paddy dike. As the engines shut down, the side door opened, and the dogs leaped out. The property looked totally abandoned. The farmhouse was empty, and the doorframe was different than the one in the frozen picture of Nachi that Bao had on his computer. Still they had the dogs search the building and the surrounding area. There were no hits, and we climbed back in. They fired the monster helicopter up, and we flew to the next location—another farmhouse ten miles away.

As we touched down, we could see people planting rice in the fields like it was a thousand years ago. There were water buffalos working the rice paddies of rectangular lakes along with a line of women, up to their knees in water, planted rice. They wore woven-reed, conical hats tied on with big, colorful ribbons. The women looked up as we were coming down, but then they went right back to planting.

A couple of farmers walked up as we were getting out of the massive machine. Bao made a big show of being friendly—the farmers were laughing. I asked Hai what he was saying.

Hai grinned and replied, "I hope we didn't scare the water buffalos."

With one look at the farmhouse, we could tell it wasn't the right one. But Bao continued his conversation with the farmers. He asked them about the tan Nissan. The farmers weren't sure what a Nissan was, but they said a tan van with windows had gone by the day before.

The dogs did a quick tour of the property, and we

got back in the air. We flew for a good fifteen minutes before the helicopter banked, turned and went into a hover. Immediately we could see that this farmhouse below was a close match to the one where Nachi was tied up; the door and frame looked the same.

When we landed, it was clear that the place was deserted. The cops took the dogs off their leashes, and they ran toward the house, sniffing the ground, running around the farmyard. One of Bao's men went over and shouldered open the front door, and the dogs raced in. Up to then, the dogs were just whimpering, but when they got inside, they went nuts, barking at a full, fierce volume at a dishtowel that was folded over the top rung of a wooden chair.

"This is the place," Bao said.

The cops started methodically tearing apart the farmhouse and the surrounding outbuildings. They dumped the contents of a trash barrel onto a big blue tarp and started going through the trash with latex gloves and tweezers. I wandered around the farm and looked into a chicken coop, a tool shed, and a pump house, which powered the irrigation system. The surrounding hills were a straw yellow; contrasting with the deep green patchwork of the paddies.

A team of cops was making plaster casts of tire tracks. I stood in the high grass and watched them work. But then I looked down and there, caught in the grass, was a business card for a creative director at Oshima Creative Force named Hiro Toma, with a handwritten note on the back that read, "Emergency/008 621 6555."

I didn't recognize the name. This was a person I had never met or worked with. For some inexplicable reason, I put the card in my pocket and did not show it to Bao.

The helicopter was going back to pick up more technicians. Hai and I got a ride back to The Nam Hai. By then the sun was going down, and the bottoms of the valleys were dark. I took the card out of my breast pocket, looked at it, and watched the last of the sunlight drop down behind the hills.

CHAPTER 24

Ever since Nachi was kidnapped, wherever we went, Hai had kept working, shooting with the GoPro and downloading all the footage we had shot from all three cameras. That night we planned on looking at it all.

We finished a late dinner in the main house. Tao came in, cleared away the dishes, and brought in a fresh pot of strong Vietnamese coffee. Then we started on the footage.

As he sat before his computer screen, Hai looked like a monk wearing white earbuds. A constantly changing array of colors crossed his face. All of a sudden, he rocked back in his chair and slammed the table with his good hand and said, "Holy God."

He turned the computer screen toward me and hit play. It was footage of the drizzly morning when we had shot in Hanoi's Old Quarter. In it, I was up ahead in a rickshaw; Nachi was in her rickshaw ten yards behind me, followed by Hai. We were all shooting, using two GoPros and my bigger Sony. We had just passed a flower shop with a giant floral display of red, white, and pink carnations right on the street. Nachi's rickshaw slowed down, and a man in a yellow raincoat walked up and spoke to her for a couple of minutes. He then turned away and looked directly at the camera Hai was shooting with. Pointing at the screen, Hai said, "Who does that look like?"

With the hooded eyes and the round, black-framed glasses, he looked exactly like the guy at the warehouse—one of the guys who had kidnapped Nachi.

"It sure looks like him," I said.

Hai said, "Christian, it looks like she knew the guy who kidnapped her. And what the hell was that guy doing in Hanoi?" I pulled out the business card and showed it to Hai. "And who the hell is this other creative director with an emergency number on his card?"

I asked Hai to play the video again. But there was nothing new to see.

For some reason, I couldn't resist. I dialed the emergency number. A computerized voice asked for my ten-digit security code. I tried back a second time, and there was silence.

The TV had been on with the sound down, but when Hai saw a "Special Report" graphic on the Nippon News Network, he turned it up.

A reporter said, "An unidentified source has released a video of what is purported to be Akio Tanaka, the Japanese colonel alleged to have ordered the Hoi An Massacre. The date and origin of this film is unknown."

The screen turned dark, and then white words appeared in Japanese, with an English translation scrolling along the bottom. It read, "The Confession of Colonel Akio Tanaka." It faded down, and a picture appeared of a very old man dressed in a black kimono, sitting on a floor close to the camera. He began speaking in Japanese with the English words appearing on the lower third of the grainy, scratched, and faded 8mm picture.

"I am Akio Tanaka," he said. "I was a colonel in the Imperial Japanese Army in the Pacific War. Since the Pacific War ended, my life has been filled with shame and sadness for the people we murdered in Indochina. I am responsible for the killing of many innocent women, men, and children from villages near Hoi An. We had been fired upon in the area. We knew these people were not the ones firing at us, but I was ordered to kill everyone anyway.

"I could have refused the order and killed myself, but I knew I would be replaced, and the order would be carried out. I did nothing except watch the slaughter of the innocent and their villages burning to the ground. I have dishonored my family and my life. The pain of my betrayal for all I believed has been with me to this day. Today it ends."

Whereupon he pulled out a short-handled dagger and committed hara-kiri. With two hands, he plunged the blade into his abdomen, drawing the blade from left to right, and then he fell forward—his blood spurting out on the screen.

CHAPTER 25

"Oh my god, oh my god, oh my god," Hai uttered under his breath, watching the last of the faded image that looked decades old.

The room was silent.

Shocked, we shut off the TV and just looked at each other. What was going on was beyond my comprehension—seeing Nachi talking to that guy on the street in Hanoi and then seeing this gruesome film of her grandfather confessing and then killing himself. Just like that—bang, bang—I did not know what to think.

"Maybe that guy on the street was someone else. The picture of him is pretty far away. A lot of people have round, black-framed glasses, and a lot have hooded eyes. We could be wrong," Hai reasoned.

"Yeah," I said, "but it is hard to believe in such a coincidence. Even though his hair was different, he looks just like Hideki Koji."

We turned the satellite TV back on, and Hai started surfing the news channels. It was like ours was the only news story in the world—with all the news channels reporting "The alleged confession of Colonel Akio Tanaka," and "The date and origin of the film is unknown," but they all played it in its entirety. A few of the news networks blacked out the blood at the end but not the sound.

Hai said, "It's like someone saved the old man's confession to crank up the drama and make sure the prime minister looks like a world-class asshole."

Hai's timer was at 25:08, twenty-five hours, eight minutes ticking down to midnight the following day. Hai switched channels. There was another report on NHK World from another "unidentified source" that a "no-confidence resolution will be put before the Japanese House of Representatives at eleven tomorrow morning. There has been no response or comment from the office of the prime minister."

The report continued. "It has also been reported that representatives of the prime minister's Liberal Democratic Party are under heavy pressure from Japanese companies with operations in Vietnam, China, and Korea to pass a no confidence vote."

I had to sleep. I had to give up my obsessive thinking and stop my mind from wildly searching to make sense out of things that made no sense at all.

In the morning, it was raining a steady downpour from a storm, which had swept in from the Gulf of Tonkin. I stood at the window, watching sheets of water come in waves. A slow drizzle would turn into a rushing monsoon in seconds, the swimming pool suddenly filling up to the rim.

Not sure if it was Tao who turned it on, but Buddhist meditation music began to flow through the room, mixing with the rush of the rain.

All this craziness surrounding Nachi made me want to better understand the Japanese—their history, their society and their inexplicable need to hide and deny the past. I started Googling and story after story popped up with one consistent theme:

"Why can't the Japanese apologize for the crimes

they committed during World War II?" Many of the stories speculated that Japan's clashes with China, Korea and Vietnam had nothing to do with wanting to enlarge fishing territories or increase mineral assets – Japan just wanted to cling to the myth that they did nothing wrong during the Pacific War.

And on those rare occasions when Japan did apologize, it came off as disingenuous and insincere.

They have offered little in reparations to its victims, and there wasn't one national shrine or memorial recognizing its slaughter and carnage of millions of men, women and children.

It has been a long history of their being unrepentant, which didn't bode well for Nachi.

I didn't know what to do with my feelings or myself. I thought of the terror in Nachi's eyes. Was she going to be the last person to die because of World War II? The Diet was going to vote in a couple of hours, and there were little more than fourteen hours to Nachi's death sentence. If they voted no confidence in the prime minister over the Hoi An Massacre, would that be enough for the kidnappers? Would they still kill her for her grandfather's sins? Would the Japanese government ever be honest with its own people?

The whole thing was in play, like some strange movie that seemed to go on forever. "The sins of the fathers" was not some dusty, biblical concept because it was happening right before my eyes. But after seeing the footage of Nachi's rickshaw in Hanoi's Old Quarter with the guy who looked like Hideki talking and smiling at her, I wondered if I was missing the whole thing, that I had everything backwards.

CHAPTER 26

At exactly eleven that morning, the Nippon News Network switched to a live shot of the combined houses of the Japanese Diet. A reporter cited the fact that "No prime minister since Kiichi Miyazawa, in 1993, has been defeated by a vote of no confidence," but many prime ministers had resigned before a vote was cast, when their poll numbers dropped or when the Diet had been deadlocked or when their popularity had been so low that the government couldn't effectively function. It was like quitting the game before you were defeated. It was about honor, respect, saving face, and lying about gigantic mass murders.

But on this day, it was all different. The resolution of no confidence passed by a wide margin, especially in the prime minister's own Liberal Democratic Party. Hours later, the prime minister and his entire cabinet resigned, while they agreed to stay on until new elections were held.

Shortly thereafter, it was announced on NHK World that a representative from the Liberal Democratic Party would address the nation at six that evening, leaving six hours until Nachi's execution. I thought the speaker might be the prime minister—who had just resigned—but what could he say after such a major defeat?

The rain continued lashing the resort; the palm trees bent almost sideways by the gale-force winds. There were mighty waves breaking on the beach, lightning bolts cracking across the sky, and ear-shattering, rolling thunder seconds later.

At seven that evening, all the networks cut to a TV studio, which was furnished like an office with two Japanese rising-sun flags on either side of a mahogany desk, with a graphic that read, "A Report to the Nation," in Japanese.

Shiro Kobayashi, the chairman of Nikkō, walked out and took his place at a podium centered in front of the desk. He spoke in a soft, yet commanding voice, his eyes drilling the camera.

"My fellow citizens," he said, "I come to you with a heavy heart, knowing our government is at a pivotal point in our country's history, where we can decide what kind of country we want to be. We all know why our prime minister and his cabinet resigned. Beyond the no-confidence vote of our Diet, it is because of the burden of lies that have finally caught up with our prime minister and with us.

"Let us face the fact that the history of our government is a litany of lies that goes well beyond the atrocities of the Pacific War and continues to this day. One needs only to look at the Fukushima Daiichi nuclear disaster, where three reactors blew up, poisoning the air, the ground, and the ocean. And our recent prime minister proclaimed to the nation that there was no health hazard.

"You all heard it: our leaders lying directly to the people in a time of danger and crisis. It is a history of lying to the Japanese people that goes back to the Pacific War. When we lost the Battle of Midway, our navy only reported the American losses, leaving out the fact that our entire carrier task force had been wiped out in our worst naval defeat in history.

"In fact, it was several months before our army found out about the defeat because the Imperial Japanese Navy had gone to great pains to hide away the survivors of the battle. The world knew—but not the Japanese people—which brings us to the most uncomfortable subject of all: the atrocities our forces committed before and during the Pacific War. The Rape of Nanking, the Bataan Death March, the Lana Massacre, the Palawan Massacre, the Wake Island Massacre, the Taiwta Massacre, the Sulug Island Massacre, and, of course, the Hoi An Massacre.

"The depravity of our forces is well known, including the thousands upon thousands of women and girls forced into sexual slavery by the Imperial Japanese Army before and during the Pacific War. In country after country, young women were abducted from their homes, only to be abused, beaten, enslaved, and killed while being called 'comfort women.'

"For once, for our country, for the Liberal Democratic Party, in front of the world, I sincerely apologize to Vietnam, to China, to Korea, to the Philippines, to Burma, to Thailand, to Malaysia, to New Guinea, to Hong Kong, and to all of what was French Indochina, for the war crimes our government has worked to minimize or completely deny. In each of these countries, we will build a memorial to the innocent people our forces murdered while we seek to make restitution to the surviving families of the millions we killed.

"We are not asking—we are demanding—that when our new government is formed, these measures shall be promptly undertaken, along with personal apologies for the unbelievable cruelty and the horrific brutality of our forces—from our new prime minister to the leaders of all the affected countries, communities, and people."

There was a big crack of lightning and more rolling thunder that seemed directly overhead.

"This is it," Hai said. "They either let her go, or they kill her."

CHAPTER 27

I called Tao, and he had a golf cart brought around, which took us to the conference center through the raging storm. We arrived totally soaked as Bao and about twenty officers were going over maps, dividing up search areas west of Hoi An.

Bao said, "There is one more place we need to look—up the Son River in the ancient Kingdom of Champa."

"It is known for the Cham ruins, with centuries-old, sacred Buddhist stupa temples. The thick jungle around there was a Vietcong stronghold, which the US heavily carpet-bombed during the war. Absolutely no one goes there because there are still land mines, unexploded bombs, and screaming ghosts that people have heard at night. If I were going to hide her, I'd go there."

When we got on the road, the rain started to back off, and we headed west through the farming areas, where we had previously landed with the military helicopter. It was at least a twenty-minute drive until we hit a dirt road, which had turned into mud. The squad car fishtailed at first, and the driver slowed down as the mud slapped against the wheel wells.

We drove up a wet steep hill and around a corner to suddenly see a booming burst of fire. A thirty-foot wall of flame was lighting up the jungle ruins with an angry red and orange glow.

Bao started pounding the steering wheel, swearing in Vietnamese – saying the equivalent of "goddammit" over and over again. "Fuck I was so stupid. I should have known they would hide here."

I wanted to throw up, feeling the crushing fear that Nachi was burning right in front of us, paying for something she had nothing to do with.

Getting out of the car, we raced up to the temple ruins, where we could feel the intense heat and the smell of gasoline forty yards away. Despite the rain, the fire roared with its acrid fumes stinging our eyes. In disbelief, I staggered closer to the flame – they had

killed Nachi and burned her body, even after they'd
gotten their goddam apology.

All at once off to the left, deep in the shadows –
there was movement. The cops pulled out their guns
and started acting like infantry. One ran right, the other
left, to outflank whatever was out there.

We were all rushing forward, toward the orange
glow of the giant bonfire, when out walked a woman
from the jungle; her face caught in the flashlight beams.
She screamed, "DON'T SHOOT! Please don't shoot
me!"

CHAPTER 28

It was Nachi.

I had never felt such a jolt of relief and happiness.

She was wet and muddy and bald, as she threw her arms around me with a long, desperate hug—taking my face in her hands and kissing me on the forehead, on my eyes, and on my lips. She then hugged Bao and the four other officers.

I asked her, "Are you okay? Are you hurt?"

"I'm okay."

We walked back to the two mud-splattered squad cars that were still running, with their doors wide open, all the lights on, and the radio squawking in Vietnamese.

I asked her, "Are the bastards still around?"

Grabbing hold of my hand, she said, "They are gone. Right up until the end, I thought they were going to throw me into the fire, but they let me run off into the jungle."

"What can you tell us about them?" Bao asked as we were getting into the back seat.

"I can tell you nothing. I wore a hood most of the time, except when they would let me eat in a dark room."

"There must be more you can tell us," Bao insisted.

"No, not now. I just want to feel safe. I want to stop feeling scared. They said they would kill my mother and my sister if I said anything. They have pictures of them on the street, with photos of where they live in Kyoto."

Bao immediately got on the car radio and ordered the other units to keep searching for the minivan, telling them that Nachi had been found but that they had to find the kidnappers. He also ordered immediate contact with the Kyoto police to get protection for Nachi's mother and sister. He handed the microphone to Nachi, and she gave the addresses and phone numbers of both women to the dispatcher on the line.

CHAPTER *29*

When we went through the gates of The Nam Hai, the whole place erupted. Both of the squad cars had their sirens going full tilt with their emergency lights on.

There were at least twenty other police cars lining the main road with all their lights and sirens on as well. Cops were out in the street, cheering and pounding on the hood of our car as we slowly drove by.

Pulling up in front of the conference center, the TV news crews swarmed our car. We got out into a tight corridor of more policemen protecting Nachi from the crowd. The wall of sound from the sirens, the cheering and clapping sent shivers through me.

The ballroom was packed. As we were taken toward

the stage, we passed hundreds of beaming Asian faces, all clapping and cheering.

As the crowd quieted, Bao began speaking in Vietnamese as Hai translated.

"This is a proud moment in the midst of a very sad story," he said. "We can say little to you now because a major investigation is currently under way. But there is still much happiness because Nachi Tanaka is here with us today."

With that, the crowd roared so loud that I thought the building might collapse.

Nachi and Bao hugged, and she walked up to the podium—her eyes shining, as were the eyes of the officers on stage with her.

"When I was imprisoned, I was locked in a dark room by myself. The entire time my captors played a television at high volume outside my door, so I could not hear their voices. But I could hear the news reports of the endless efforts so many made to find me, to save my life.

"My deepest, most heartfelt thanks to the Hoi An police, the Vietnamese people and the people of Japan for affecting my release and for allowing the truth of what happened here in Hoi An to be known."

The crowd clapped so loudly that I felt light headed from the dizzying joy of the moment.

Bao wanted Nachi to see The Nam Hai's doctor, but she refused. "I just want to go back to my room and take a hot shower."

Even though they provided us with a golf cart, the three of us decided to just walk back to the compound. A couple of news crews tried to follow us, but two Hoi An cops turned them around. After all the noise, the silence of the evening was deafening as we walked through the gates of the compound.

Hai said, "I must call my wife and talk to my son. They have been worried sick. I'll see you later."

CHAPTER *30*

Nachi said quietly, "I can't believe I'm back here. I can't believe you found me; and all the people at those factories putting their jobs on the line."

"It was incredible," I said. "All those people walking out."

She went into her house, and I went to find Tao. He was watching the news on TV in the main house. It was all in Vietnamese and kept cutting back and forth from the reporter to showing shots of Nachi getting out of the squad car and speaking on stage; then shots of Bao, of all the policemen, and of the crowd going crazy.

"Tao, we could use some food. Ask Nachi and Hai too; you can order for me."

All of a sudden, Bao, with a swarm of detectives and technicians descended on the courtyard.

Bao said, "We need the clothes she's wearing and a DNA sample. The hotel put some other clothes she can wear in her closet."

"You tell her." I don't know why I felt impatient.

"Gladly," Bao said as he walked over and knocked on her door.

I went back to my place, showered, shaved, and put on a pair of jeans and a clean work shirt, then returned to the main house where Tao had laid out a feast to celebrate Nachi's safe return.

Hai came in with a smiling Nachi wearing a white V-neck sweater, bright-green silk slacks, and wedge sandals.

A few minutes later, Bao walked in and sat down with us at the table. Turning to Nachi, he said, "You must tell us more of what happened. You were with them for over a week; you were moving around with them. You must remember a lot more."

"Can't this wait?" I asked. "She's exhausted."

"I can tell you that they never mistreated me," Nachi said. "They were polite. When we traveled in the van, they wore surgical masks and black baseball caps or hooded sweatshirts. One person did all the talking, but it was minimal at that, like asking me what I liked to eat."

"But didn't they ever talk about what they were doing?" I asked. "They could have been shot by the police. They still could be."

"That's right," Bao said, looking across the table and straight into her eyes.

"From what I could understand, they were student idealists," Nachi continued. "Once, the guy who talked said that they wanted to expose the lies of the Japanese government and that grabbing me was the only way the truth of the Hoi An Massacre would be acknowledged. I didn't think they were going to kill me. But I spent so much time alone in the dark that I started to go a little crazy, and the fear started creeping in. Right up to when they set the temple on fire."

Bao reinforced, "Tonight I want you to think very hard about what you experienced; even the smallest detail is important."

He got up and added, "There has to be more that you are not telling us." With that, he walked out.

I finished my meal in silence, trying not to believe that Bao might be right.

CHAPTER *31*

It was almost midnight when we finished eating, and I was bone-tired. As Nachi and I crossed the courtyard, we heard the sound of running outside the walls. Cops in full military battle dress, carrying submachine guns, were patrolling the grounds with two German shepherds. Down on the beach more police were moving out guests from the compounds next door.

"What's going on? Nachi asked. "Why all the police?"

"I don't know. It looks like they're putting a big guard around the compound. We'll find out soon enough. Just go inside and lock your door."

Minutes later, Bao was at my door carrying two

AK-47 assault rifles and a canvas bag loaded with clips.

"What's going on? Why do we need all this?" I asked pointing at the weapons.

Bao set them down on the dining table. "I just talked with a Tokyo police organized-crime detective. He told me that four very bad, convicted yakuza hit men flew from Tokyo to Da Nang yesterday. He said they were people who they watched constantly and are from the worst of the worst of the yakuza clans— the Hamaguma family. Next to them, your American mafia look like children. They're into everything from corporate extortion to murder, and they have a long alliance with right-wing nationalist politicians. The word is that when the prime minister resigned, many people lost a lot of yen from cancelled contracts for work on the nuclear power plants.

"We don't know exactly why they are in the area. But they are here, and we have to believe it has something to do with Ms. Tanaka's release. They are professional killers, so we want to be ready if they do come here."

He looked directly at me, "You do know how to fire an AK, don't you? I looked you up. You were in the US Marines. You were at Hue City."

"Yes, I was."

It was the last thing I expected to do when I returned to Vietnam. I'd put that life behind me. But here I was—holding an AK again and it felt all too familiar.

After a long pause, Bao said, "I must show you where we have our people so that we don't have problems with friendly fire."

Hai joined us as we walked the police perimeter that had been created around the compound. There were high stone walls on three sides, but the fourth side was all glass and totally exposed to the ocean. It was about seventy-five yards to the water's edge.

I could tell that Bao had been in the military, because he had built a mutually supporting defense that was set up with clear lines of fire. His guys dug foxholes in the bushes and there were several men on the roof, both front and back—all in black, with helmets and night-vision goggles. Bao also had the road to the compound blocked off, with four squad cars and more cops dug into foxholes on either side of the drive. These guys were serious.

"They could come from anywhere," he said. "These are very experienced killers. They have been known to blow up a block of buildings to kill one man in a car and then go on to kill his family."

It was past midnight when I got back to Nachi's and she was asleep. The house was mainly one large, open space for living, dining, and sleeping, with a big couch up against the bottom of the bed, and floor-to-ceiling, sliding glass doors—all facing the ocean. The curtains were drawn and all the outside lights had been shut off.

I picked up the assault rifle, pulled the clip, and opened the breach. Everything looked correct. I checked the clip to see if it was full.

Bao had also given me a police radio with an earpiece. There was some chatter in Vietnamese, but beyond that, it was quiet. I sat with the gun on the couch in the dark and waited. A half hour later, I heard Nachi's voice in the darkness saying, "I'm sorry you've had to go through this. It is my family story. I am so ashamed to have brought our misery into your life."

I could only see her shadow in the dark.

"You know," she said, "I loved my grandfather as a little girl. When I was four or five, he would take me along shopping. We had a little two-wheeled wire cart to hold the food. I would pull the cart when it was empty, and he would pull it back when it was full. We'd go into all the little shops. Everyone knew him, liked him. We'd buy vegetables, fish, and rice. Every time we would stop at a toy store on the way home, and he would let me pick out a small toy. Paper dolls, a little car, a tiny action figure. I loved the paper dolls the most. I would give them names.

"It wasn't until after high school, after he had committed hara-kiri, that I read his diary, where he'd written about all the horrible things. I still have the diary. It is in a safety-deposit box in Tokyo."

Here she was, this lovely voice in the darkness, filled with fear. I could hear the cops speaking quietly on the radio in Vietnamese. I couldn't understand them, but there was no tension in their voices.

After a half hour, Nachi said, "You should go to sleep. You can't stay up all night."

I said, "Don't worry. I've done this before."

I didn't include the part about waiting in the dark, scared it was my last night on earth, which I'd done before as well.

CHAPTER **32**

I could see a faint light in the sky through cracks in the shutters. Nachi was still sleeping. I wanted to take a shower and put on fresh clothes. Quietly I opened the side door and was nearly shot by one of Bao's men on a walking patrol. It was a shock to the system—the guy raising his gun and getting ready to fire.

After getting cleaned up, I walked back to Nachi's house. She was standing by the bed, wearing a very slim, white satin slip and a lacy white bra with lots of overflowing cleavage. I was speechless. She was impossibly beautiful. Nachi acted like there nothing unusual about it.

She asked, "Are you okay?"

"Yeah, I'm fine."

"Well, I'm going to take a shower."

She walked into the bathroom and closed the door. As the shower started running, I heard a phone buzzing. I looked through a pile of Nachi's clothes and found an iPhone with a text message that read, "Call emergency number now. 008 359 3742."

There it was, staring me right in the face.

I called the number and got the same computerized voice asking for a ten-digit security code. I went outside and sat by the long koi pond in the courtyard, but I couldn't stop thinking about the guy with the round, black-framed glasses, coming up to her in Hanoi's Old Quarter.

Hai came up behind me and said, "Bao just called. They found Hideki Koji and his roommate, Kei Ichiro."

"Really?"

"Yeah, they had both been shot in the head. They'd been tortured and dumped in a tan minivan, down by the river."

"Jesus fucking Christ! I think it's time we had a

serious talk with Nachi," I said. "Why don't you go get your laptop and I'll call her over."

When Nachi came in, Hai and I were already sitting around the coffee table as he fired up his computer.

I said, "Nachi, I want you to look at this footage that we took in Hanoi, in the Old Quarter."

She watched the video.

"We think you know this man by the way he is smiling and talking to you," I said to her.

"Are you kidding? He asked for directions. I told him the park was one block up and to the right."

"Well, we think that the guy you were talking to was one of the people who abducted you in Hoi An. His name is Hideki Koji. Both he and his roommate were murdered last night, after being tortured."

When I said that, her head snapped back several inches, like she'd been punched. She blinked her eyes rapidly and looked down at her hands. "I can't believe it. Why? They didn't hurt me. They let me go. Who would do that?"

"Maybe it's the people who lost millions when the

prime minister had to resign. He was their guy, and now they might be coming for you, for wrecking everything with your grandfather's story," I said.

She hung her head and held her hands together.

"Now look at this." I handed her Creative Director Hiro Toma's business card.

"Where did you get this?" she asked.

"You know where I got it."

Nachi said nothing.

"Who is he?" I pushed.

"I worked for him at Oshima doing Mazda commercials. He gave it to me to use if I had a problem on a shoot."

"What is the security code?"

"Zero, followed by one through nine. It was simple, so I could remember it. But it never worked. The line went dead when I tried it."

"Did you have two phones with you?"

"Yes, one for business and one for personal matters. They took one from me, but the other was back here."

She looked up at Hai and then me. "But why would they kill those two students?"

"Revenge," Hai said. "They're the same people who think that even after this Asian holocaust, the only thing Japan did wrong in the Second World War was lose the war. And there are plenty of them still around."

CHAPTER 33

Right then, Bao walked in with two cops in full military dress, each with a submachine gun slung over his right shoulder.

"The Kyoto Police have your mother and sister under protection," Bao said. "But we are very concerned about what will happen here tonight. If they come, I guess they will come with the darkness. So I suggest you get as much rest as possible because nobody is going to sleep tonight.

"I want you all to move to Hai's house. It is closer to the sidewalls and easier to defend. We plan on getting you out of here tomorrow morning. This is the best location to defend if they do come tonight."

Bao and his men left, and we all moved over to Hai's house. Nachi called her mother. They spoke in Japanese for a half hour. Sitting on a couch in the corner, Nachi mainly listened to her mother and occasionally spoke with a quiet voice.

When she got off the phone, she smiled, "My mother is fine. She is playing cards with a woman police officer who is staying in the apartment with her. The officer has been winning. They're playing for buttons."

She called her sister, Kiki, who worked for a public relations firm in Kyoto and lived with her husband and two kids in the suburbs. As they chatted back and forth in Japanese, they made happy sounds, like there was nothing serious going on. All while they had a Kyoto police cruiser parked outside Kiki's front door.

After that, she called the British creative team from Oshima. She spoke in English with a clear, posh British accent. I wondered where the heck that had come from; it was like she just turned it on.

She said, "It was the most harrowing thing I've ever been through, and now the police think we are still in danger from the people who came down here and killed two of the people who were holding me."

She listened and then said, "We are leaving here tomorrow, but as of now, I don't know where we will go. Thank you for your concern and support. And the *blank check*."

Tao brought in some simple Vietnamese comfort food, *Bún cha* rice with pork and spring rolls, and we had a late-afternoon meal. Eating in silence, we passed around the dishes like it was communion. Tao ate with us. Out of the window, I could see a couple of Bao's men lugging a machine gun and ammo across the front lawn. The assailants could come from anywhere—the ocean, the back walls, or straight down the road with a car bomb.

The sun started going down, but the resort's lights remained off on the southern end where we were. As the night moved in, we were left with sounds of the surf, the occasional bird cawing, and a cacophony of insects chirping, whirring, and buzzing in the distance—going off and on like blinking lights.

CHAPTER *34*

We sat in the darkness and waited. Time felt frozen. I tried to stop looking at my watch. It was almost one in the morning when two big explosions went off along the wall by the driveway to the compound entrance.

"Get in the bathroom!" I yelled at Nachi. "And lie down in the tub."

I could hear the chatter on the radio, but Bao's people weren't firing. Hai was hunkered down right beside me.

I instinctively thought it was a diversion. Someone had thrown a couple of hand grenades over the twenty-foot back wall, and Bao's guys weren't buying it either. They quietly held their positions. I opened the sliding door and crawled through the opening. I could see shadows of the men in four foxholes positioned every twenty yards along the rear of the property, facing the beach and the ocean.

It was then that a rocket-propelled grenade hit the glass wall of the main house and exploded inside, setting the place on fire. The guys on the roof were walking around, but they had to jump off before the flames reached them. But first they fired off a series of illumination rounds that made it look like noon on the moon.

Instantly we could see them coming through the winking silver light. Ten guys driving five ATVs barreled down the beach, a hundred yards away. A heavy machine gun on the far right opened up with at least six other guys firing assault rifles. The ATV on the left side blew up into a fireball.

The illumination rounds started dying, the light quickly fading. The other ATVs were stopped, and soon all we could see were the flashes of them firing at us and the one vehicle burning.

What I didn't know was that Bao had a quick-reaction force in reserve that was off to the left of the attackers. Originally I had thought we were dealing with the four guys from Tokyo. But there were many more, and they were closing in fast. Hai and I got ready for them. Bao had told us not to fire unless they got in close.

They came in with an all-out banzai charge, their guns on full automatic. It was a completely reckless attack going straight into the teeth of Bao's defense. When they were thirty yards out, our quick-reaction force hit them from the left flank with heavy, small-arms fire, which was followed by a shower of hand grenades. Hai and I lay on the floor in the dark, in front of the open sliding doors, searching the darkness for movement.

I yelled in the direction of the bathroom. "Nachi, are you okay?"

"I am. Is it safe?"

"No! It's not. Stay in the tub, and keep your head down."

There was still shooting going on. Two of Bao's guys dragged a prisoner up from the sand to the lawn. The prisoner was Vietnamese. The cops started screaming at him. The prisoner cowered and said nothing. One of the cops pulled out a 9mm automatic and shot him in the knee; the prisoner screamed in agony. The cop put the same 9mm in the prisoner's mouth and continued yelling at him.

The prisoner started talking a blue streak. Hai listened for several minutes and then told me what he was saying.

"He says he is Vietnamese mafia from Hanoi and that they'd been hired by the Japanese yakuza and there were twenty guys in total—four Japanese and sixteen Vietnamese."

Bent over low, Bao and two of his men came running across the lawn. The main house was completely engulfed in flames.

"Are you okay?" he asked us.

"Yeah. What happened?"

"We killed eight. Plus we have the prisoner, but one escaped down the beach. They were pretty brave, but they were mighty stupid. Where's Nachi?"

"In the bathtub."

"Keep her there. Don't let your guard down. There

are still ten of them out there."

They dragged the prisoner over next to the sidewall and continued questioning him despite the fact he was writhing in pain. The cop who had shot him pointed the automatic right between his eyes, and the prisoner started screaming in garbled Vietnamese.

"He said they're coming with the fire trucks. They've got two Red Cross-marked ambulances. One has a bomb," Hai repeated.

We could hear sirens. Bao called his guys at the front gate to stop them. But the fire trucks and the ambulances had already gone through the gate, and the main house fire was spreading to the other buildings. Several cops started to move the squad cars to let the fire engines through.

Bao screamed in Vietnamese on his radio, "Keep the road blocked. There's a bomb in one of the ambulances."

A wild, confused firefight began in the dark. The real firemen ran for their lives, and Bao's guys raked the ambulances with bursts of automatic fire.

The second ambulance blew up like it had been hit

with an artillery shell, sending up a fireball fifty feet in the air, which lit up the entire scene. Both vehicles were shredded and burning; the second ambulance's roof was caught in the branches of a palm tree. Two of Bao's guys had been hit by shrapnel and were being worked on. Another policeman dragged a wounded but alive prisoner away from the fire.

CHAPTER *35*

We were evacuated to the main reception building. We could see the fire raging at the far end of the road as more fire trucks, with sirens screaming and lights flashing, rolled in from Da Nang.

Directed to a suite of windowless rooms, the three of us sat in the living room and just silently stared at each other.

Hai flopped down on the couch. Nachi and I sat in armchairs. The place was hot and stuffy. I turned on the AC.

"All that was to kill me?" Nachi asked.

"Yeah," I said. "And I think you know why."

"Because I told my grandfather's story?"

"Yeah," I replied. "You cost a lot of people a lot of money. Millions upon millions. Companies like Tokyo Energy and Power, the people responsible for Fukushima, and the gangsters with their lucrative construction bribes. Those guys had bought and paid for the prime minister—a huge investment. And I'm sure they feel totally fucked over. For them, it was like you staged a coup, and their guy took the fall."

There was a silence that lasted ages.

"Well, it's true," Nachi stated, just like that, nodding her head. "It's true."

Hai had his good arm over his eyes, lying flat on the couch, his sling across his chest. He rose up, "What the hell do you mean?"

"The whole thing was an Oshima production," she revealed. "From start to finish. We did it just like a commercial. The hara-kiri scene with the old man was shot at a production studio in Tokyo. The crazy social media surge, the flash mob in Tokyo, the "unidentified" sources—it was all orchestrated by us."

"Are you kidding me? You're not seriously telling

me this whole thing was an act?" I interrupted.

"Um, well, yes, it was."

"And we were your fucking pawns?" I yelled. "You weren't the only one, Nachi. They were going to kill us all tonight. They still might."

"I am so sorry ... so, so sorry. I thought it was the right thing to do. The confession was real. My mother kept it from me—until years later when I was cleaning a bookcase and I found my grandfather's diary hidden behind a false back. It was all there, Christian. Hoi An and many other terrible events, where thousands were slaughtered—and the confession is word for word."

"What? Are you fucking kidding me?" I shouted. "You just about destroyed our lives because you felt guilty about what your grandfather did. And you needed some usable actors in your play. This isn't a game, Nachi. People have risked their lives for you. I hate your guts."

She sat stunned and then speaking softly, "I detested the size of the lie. I hated the prime minister for his denials, and there were many Oshima clients who hated the relations he kept destroying. With China, with Korea, with Vietnam. There are still twenty million ghosts that won't go away."

"The guilt of your grandfather and the interests of Oshima's clients? This is what you fucking risked our lives for? You can go straight to hell."

Nachi pleaded, "No one would have cared if we had just showed the diary. The story of the Hoi An Massacre was always ignored. We had to bring it to life. We had to speak to people's hearts."

"With a staged abduction and the overthrow of the government?"

Lowering her eyes, she quietly responded, "Yes."

"I ought to give you to Bao right now," I said, "and you can go rot in a Vietnamese jail for the rest of your life."

"Yes, you could do that," she answered.

Hai said, "I don't think we should say a thing. It will get a lot worse if this gets out."

I couldn't stop. I continued shouting at her. "You realize that you got those two students murdered? They were tortured. Tortured!"

She was crying. "I never thought they would

retaliate or that they'd figure it out. It was all based on the truth."

I looked at her. "And you hung it around their necks."

"Yes."

Hai said, "We need to rest. We need to think, and above all we need to get out of here."

I was still so mad at Nachi that I didn't know what to do. Hai slept on the couch. Nachi and I each took a bedroom. I tried to meditate, to clear my head of the confusion of lies upon lies. Trying to think about nothing but my breathing, I finally drifted off.

CHAPTER *36*

Bao had us awakened late in the morning. They were moving us to the airport for a flight to Hanoi. We took turns in the bathroom and got dressed. Tao brought in a pot of hot coffee and a cold meal of fresh fruit, cheese, and rice crackers.

I was still so pissed off at Nachi that I couldn't see straight. Then she walked in wearing a gold hijab headscarf that framed her face and covered her baldness and the upper part of her chest. Underneath that, she wore a blue turquoise blouse, jeans, and white heels. And soft-pink lipstick that shone like chrome.

"Are you going to turn me in?"

"No," I conceded. "But you must realize the yakuza killers know everything. I am sure that they tortured every last word out of those students. And your friends at Oshima could be in big trouble too. How much did the students know?"

"Most everything. They were in on the planning with the creative director whose business card you found."

"Hiro Toma?"

"Yes, he was in charge of the project. His attitude was that we were doing an important job for our country."

"And for your clients."

"Yes."

Bao had assembled six identical Hoi An squad cars out front. He looked extremely serious.

"We had a long talk with the prisoners, and they were kind enough to tell us that the attack was mounted by Truong Van, the head of the Hanoi mafia. The Japanese paid them $5 million in US dollars, which the yakuza brought with them in suitcases. We think we got them all last night, but we are concerned about our drive to the Da Nang airport. There could be more of them waiting for us along the way."

Bao put us in the back seat of one of the cars and had us lie down as we drove out of the resort. He had all six cars drive out of The Nam Hai at once and split up into three two-car units, each going a different way to the airport.

We headed west, and the two cars ahead of us went straight north on the coast road. It was usually a twenty-minute drive, but we drove way west before turning north for the airport.

It was open countryside. We sat up and watched the endless number of rice paddies go by. But then out the window, several miles to the east, we saw a huge gray mushroom cloud go up, followed by Bao's radio exploding with voices screaming in Vietnamese.

Hai yelled, "They hit the first two cars with an IED. They were driving too close together. Everyone was killed."

Bao told the driver to pour it on, but I could tell he was deeply shaken. These were his men. Bao closed his eyes, and it looked like he was praying. We pulled into the Vietnam Airlines terminal and were escorted by airport police to a lounge on the second floor. Sitting in a section behind a bamboo screen, we were joined by four of Bao's detectives dressed in street clothes. They looked awful, the soul-sapping shock of a huge loss all over their gaunt faces.

In the corner a television was silently running a Tokyo news channel; English subtitles ran on the lower third of the screen. I saw a picture of Oshima's Tokyo headquarters and started reading the words on the screen.

"In business news today, two employees of Oshima Advertising were killed in separate incidents yesterday. Hiro Toma, a creative director at Oshima, drowned in a diving accident while vacationing on Australia's Great Barrier Reef. In a second, unrelated incident, a technician at Oshima Special Effects, Kiro Ma, fell to his death from his apartment balcony some time between two and three in the morning."

Nachi and Hai were reading right along with me. The cops weren't watching. I could feel the fear rising in me, going from my feet to my legs, chest, and heart. I locked eyes with Nachi and went over to sit next to her.

I whispered, "Who was the technician?"

She whispered back, "The guy who ran all the

special effects. He did all the tricks with the blood and making the film look old."

"They know everything for sure."

CHAPTER 37

W e flew to Hanoi in another Vietnam Airlines 737. They put us up front with Bao, and his four detectives sat beside and behind us. It was dark when we landed. Guided off the plane by Hanoi airport police, we walked down a steel stairway to the tarmac, where we were loaded into a stretched van with blacked-out windows.

We rode into Hanoi—Hai's hometown—in silence. It was dark and rainy. The tires hissed through the water, the wipers slapping, barely keeping up with the rain.

Pulling up to the Opera Wing's side entrance of the Metropole, we were hustled inside the hotel under a black awning and into a hallway, where we were greeted by the general manager of the hotel.

"We welcome you back to the Metropole," he said, "where our entire staff stands ready to serve and assist you in any way that is needed." He added with clear sincerity, "You are heroes to us and the Vietnamese people. Our hotel's security service has protected presidents, kings, movie stars, and prime ministers. You can expect the highest level of attention and safety."

We were taken in a private elevator up to the fourth floor, where the door opened to a large, private reception area. Security guards in slim-fit business suits, with earpieces and stern looks on their faces took us down the hall to a door with a brass plaque that read "Imperial Suite"—the most exclusive residence in the hotel. The manager opened the door with a flourish.

"Consider this your home. This suite has hosted many of the most famous people in the world, but none more important than you."

"We thank you," Bao said. "But we just want to be invisible as long as we're here."

The manager toured us around the unbelievably lavish rooms which had a dining area, a fully stocked bar, a library and conference room, a magnificent bathroom with a gold-leaf bathtub and Bose surround sound throughout the entire suite.

"All the rooms have bulletproof windows, which were installed when President Clinton came for a visit."

"Thank you, President Clinton," I said to myself.

The general manager put his hand to his earpiece and listened. He said to Bao, "The chief of the Hanoi police has arrived, and he wants to come up and meet you."

"Absolutely not," said Bao. "I don't want him near this place or talking to our people."

Bao looked at me and said, "This guy heads up one of the most corrupt police forces in Vietnam. They do a lot of bad things here—things that we'd never do in Hoi An."

Bao turned back to the general manager and said, "Tell the police chief that we are tired and that we will not be able to meet with him tonight. Now, if you'll excuse us, I want to talk to your head of security. I don't want to see Hanoi police anywhere around here or in the park next door."

Within minutes, the Metropole's security chief arrived at the Imperial Suite. He looked like an Asian

George Clooney, with black slicked-back hair, wearing a blue Armani suit and black wing tips. His name was An Dung, which Hai told me meant "peaceful hero." We sat in the large conference room with seating for twenty.

Bao told An Dung that he totally distrusted the Hanoi police, "We know for a fact that the police are in bed with the local mafia."

An Dung brushed an invisible piece of lint off his suit. "You're correct. The police steal from the people every day. There are many cab drivers who have told me of being stopped several times in a day for phony violations. They used to charge one hundred thousand dong, about six US dollars. Now they're charging the drivers two hundred thousand dong. They take all their money. They are vultures."

He went on by saying, "They also extort all the shopkeepers in our Old Quarter. In many places, the cops have the mafia do the collections. What are people to do? Go to the police? They will burn their shop down in a second. But that's just the little stuff. Where they make millions is in construction. They can shut down any project unless a company is willing to pay bribes on everything—concrete, steel, glass, interiors, labor, cranes. The cops and our mafia are like an octopus strangling our economy."

Bao asked, "We need a way to get in and out of here without being seen. Can you help us with that?"

"Yes, I can," An Dung said. "You have heard of the bomb shelter that was built under the hotel's swimming pool?"

"Yes," Bao said.

"Well, there is also a tunnel that very few know about. It runs from under the hotel to an office building two blocks away. It's called the Mistress Tunnel, as it is occasionally used to bring in women for our special guests who want to keep a low profile."

The security chief left, and the eight of us stayed sitting around the conference table.

Bao said, "Our target is Truong Van. He's the big mafia man here in Hanoi and the one behind the attack and the killing of our officers. He is reputed to be the emperor of the Old Quarter, and he's feared by everyone including the police. We must find him first and then neutralize his protection."

"Are you going to arrest him?" I asked.

"No," Bao said. "We're going to kill him ... possibly while resisting arrest. He killed our men, and we're going to take him out. He could buy his way out of almost anything here. We'll save him the trouble."

The room was chillingly quiet for several minutes; then I stood up and said, "What if ... we do what we're good at? We could stage a tourism commercial in the Old Quarter and put on a traditional Dragon Dance parade with lots of fireworks—cause a big distraction. It's a real part of Vietnamese culture. It symbolizes blessings and prosperity that expel devils and brings good luck."

Not getting any pushback, I continued, "So we go to Truong Van for permission to shoot on the streets of his neighborhood. We'll offer to pay his people to be in it, and of course we'll pay him, like fifty grand."

"How are you going to finance that?" Bao questioned.

"Remember, we have a *blank check* from our friends at Oshima."

Bao considered the idea, "Truong doesn't know that we know it was them. He should be thinking that we killed all their men and that we know little. The prisoners have been listed as dead."

Nachi started texting, then looking up from her cell phone, "Well, it can be done. I know producers here in Hanoi who can come up with giant dragons, along with the actors and musicians. But who is going to contact Truong Van?"

"I will," I suggested. "They know nothing about me, except that I'm in Vietnam to shoot tourism commercials."

Hai spoke up, "I want to go home. My wife has been sick with worry. I want to see my little boy. It's not far from here."

Turning to him, I responded, " Listen Hai, I know this isn't what you signed up for. You have a wife, a kid and I totally understand if we end it all here. You don't have to come with us."

"No, Christian, this is no longer just about Nachi," Hai said. "It's about the suffering of our ancestors— mine, Lan's, Bao's," then pointing to the four officers, "and their's. I'm coming back. I'm going with you."

Bao called An Dung's direct number and explained what we needed. In minutes, two security guards were at the door. They gave Hai a floppy canvas hat and an oversized raincoat and took him down the private elevator to the Mistress Tunnel.

CHAPTER *38*

What the fuck was I doing? Here we were planning for a Vietnamese Dragon Dance, as cover for killing Hanoi's mafia chief, his lieutenants, and his bodyguards. I couldn't believe it. I was in so deep. I was all in, but in many ways, there was no choice. The yakuza had been paid a lot of money to kill Nachi. They weren't stopping. Like an awful dream, it was feeling like Hue City. Kill or be killed.

Bao was right. If we were serious about staying alive, we'd have to take them out. The Hanoi police certainly weren't going to help. We were on our own.

Bao and his men were put up in rooms down the hall. Nachi and I sat in the library and watched the footage that we had shot in the Old Quarter. The shops, the crazy traffic, and then this amazing scene at the intersection of five main streets. In the center of the intersection, like a public fountain, was a new white Jaguar XJ supercharged sedan that was parked with no one in it. The traffic flowing all around it.

"Who in Hanoi would have the power to park that car there?" I asked.

"Yeah," Nachi said. "Who would have that much nerve?"

"I'd bet money that's Truong Van's car. We should talk to Bao and see if we can find out for certain."

Nachi had ordered lunch—banana blossom salads, bird nest soup and steamed beef rolls from room service, which the hotel security guards delivered. We sat and ate dinner at the marble island in the middle of the suite's elaborate kitchen.

Nachi said, "Christian, I don't expect you to forgive me for what I have done. I know what I have put you through—like you said, like an actor in my play."

There was a long, strained silence.

"Our family was haunted by the Hoi An story," she continued. "My grandfather lived in shame. My mother could not get over the memory of all the people who were killed. And then after years of knowing, I thought it was time to remember those who had died and been murdered and forgotten.

"And Oshima was the way to do it. So many clients hated the prime minister's lying about the past and offending all the countries where we had killed millions."

I could hear the living room clock ticking from across the room.

CHAPTER **39**

A security guard brought up a choice of wigs to the suite for Nachi to try on as her disguise.

Bao sent two of his detectives out to the Old Quarter dressed as cable-company repairmen. They had a small van for scouting out the five-way intersection where we had seen the white Jaguar sedan. Later we found out that they were able to install a pole cam, twenty feet off the ground, on a streetlight; it would record everything that happened at the five-way intersection for forty-eight hours.

Even though it was late, Nachi put in calls to assemble a shooting crew, fireworks, drummers, dragon dancers, and of course, dragons.

Winding down, we sat in the suite's bar and made

drinks, slicing up limes and making Tanqueray and tonics in tall frosted-green glasses. I turned on the stereo system, which immediately began filling the room with light baroque music.

We sat on the couch together sipping our gin and tonics. I could feel the tension leaving my body.

"I may not have told you, but I speak four languages," she said as she counted down on her fingers. "English, Japanese, Vietnamese and...of course, body language," she smiled with light in her eyes.

I laughed. It was so unexpected, like we were back in Hong Kong, without a worry in the world. I loved her beauty and her charismatic charm. But I hated her for all the lies, the two dead students, the four dead Hoi An cops, the dead Oshima guys, and for getting us nearly killed. And now we were getting ready to murder a bunch of criminals with an equal chance that they would kill us first. It was a cold, stinging shower and a long way from Hong Kong.

Even after a second drink, I was stone sober. I kept thinking about how to lure out Truong Van and make him part of the filming, then shoot him. Blow his car up. Or burn his house down with him in it. It wasn't hard. I knew how to turn a few propane tanks into a bomb, which could knock down a good-sized building.

It was like Hue. Being unable to sleep in a foxhole in the dark while trying to figure out how to kill the guys who were killing us.

Getting up from the couch. "I have to sleep. And Nachi, you've got to ask yourself if you're ready for this. We could get you on a plane tomorrow. Bao doesn't know the real story. We could send you to the United States or to Paris with protection. We still have Oshima's *blank check*."

"No, we have to go back to Japan; this is where all the strings are being pulled, and where the lies were created."

"Yeah, but we've got to live through Hanoi first."

CHAPTER *40*

Dressed as cable-repair guys, Bao sent his two detectives to continue scouting the Old Quarter. The cover allowed them to go down alleys and get up on top of buildings, where the cable television lines were strung, as they made their way toward Truong Van's house and his organization. It was a block away and down a long alley from the five-way intersection where we were staging the Dragon Dance. A stand-alone, white-stucco house with its own small park and perfectly maintained flower beds.

They were stopped by a couple of guys with ponytails, leather jackets, and ugly attitudes who said in Vietnamese, "This is private property. No one is allowed back here without permission."

Bao's men told them they were just checking the

TV cables and that they'd had reports of problems. The ponytail guys seemed to buy their story since they were wearing genuine, stolen uniforms from Hanoi's largest cable provider and carried testing gear to measure a cable's signal strength.

They put up ladders and tested several cables in the alley before moving on to where a feeder cable entered Truong Van's house. The ponytail guys ignored them, spending their time smoking cigarettes and joking around. The detectives then installed a device that would monitor the Internet and telephone conversations running through the cable, broadcasting to a recording van a couple of blocks away.

Back at the Metropole, Bao called a meeting in the library conference room. "The Japanese are not the only ones with underworld connections in Hanoi. I do too. I have a friend whom I arrested years ago in Hoi An. I got his charges dropped after he gave us some good information, and we have stayed in touch. He is the one who provided the uniforms, the van, and the equipment. More importantly, he is very familiar with Truong Van's operation."

Bao continued, "Here is what we know. Truong Van is one of the most heavily protected people in Hanoi.

He travels with a minimum of four bodyguards and never meets with anyone he does not know or trust.

"He only communicates through his lieutenants. My friend suggested we meet with a man named Quoc Huy, who is his chief enforcer in the Old Quarter. He operates out of a restaurant and bar at the corner of Ta Hien and Luong Nqoc Quten. It's a sports bar, where they gamble on games. It's called Mr. X's.

"He told me that the white Jaguar is Truong Van's main transportation and that it is heavily armored.

"As a rule, he runs everything out of his house. There are always guards outside when he is present. No one is allowed near the place without being stopped."

It was decided that Hai and I would go to Mr. X's that afternoon and see if we could talk with Quoc Huy about shooting our "commercial" in the Old Quarter.

You always think of these vicious, powerful mafia guys as larger-than-life characters. So it was a real disappointment to meet this little man wearing a cheap silk suit, with a ridiculous comb-over and missing teeth.

We talked with him at the bar with thirty flat-panel

television sets behind us, broadcasting sporting events from around the world—everything from cricket, to sumo wrestling, to homing-pigeon races. Hai explained that we were shooting a tourism commercial and that we wanted to enlist his help in getting permission to film in the Old Quarter the next day.

Hai gave him a gift of $1,000 in US dollars, to show our sincerity and respect. He liked that. He signaled the bartender to make us drinks. Hai started telling him how we wanted to close one main street and the five-way intersection. We needed to lay one hundred yards of dolly tracks down the street, and we needed three hundred extras for the crowd scenes.

He nodded thoughtfully.

Hai translated for Quoc Huy, "We have done many movies here before, but it costs millions of dong to do these things."

Hai told him we were prepared to pay $50,000 in US dollars—cash— for the services of his organization. He nodded his head again. Getting a pad from the bar, he wrote down Hai's cell phone number and said in Vietnamese, "I'll get back to you."

CHAPTER *41*

Hai and I headed back to the Metropole the long way. The streets were crowded. It was impossible to tell if anyone was following us. We walked across the green, leafy park next to the Metropole, where brides were photographed in their bright white wedding dresses all the time, practically day and night. It was a Hanoi tradition to have your wedding picture taken in front of the Metropole and the statues in the park across the street.

At the corner of Tong Dan and Le Phung Hien was an office building, where we took the elevator to the basement. There we met a Metropole security guard who unlocked a steel door to the Mistress Tunnel, which led us back to the hotel.

It wasn't long before Hai got a call from the mafia

enforcer from Mr. X's. His boss liked the deal and they could provide the services we'd discussed, and that they would pay for street permits and the extras out of the $50,000. Hai told him our crews would arrive at six in the morning to start setting up and that we'd like to have a short street party to thank the neighborhood when we were done.

Hai told him in Vietnamese, "Please invite your boss. We'll bring the money in cash."

"U.S.?"

"Yes, U.S. dollars."

That night we all sat down together—Bao, his four men, Nachi, Hai, and me. We were it. Bao's criminal buddy was helping with logistics, but it was up to us to make it work. We went over the plan again and again. We had a big, blown-up Google map of the Old Quarter, marking the streets we were going to block off, the five-way intersection, the alley, and Truong's white house. Even though it was happening on a Saturday morning, the shoot would cause massive gridlock.

This went on for several hours in the conference room. There was a big concern that Truong Van would not be curious enough to want to see a big movie shoot in his neighborhood, that it might not be interesting enough for him.

Knowing we were going to attack in the morning and people were going to die, one way or another—made it very hard to sleep. Nachi went to her room, and I drank a bottle of expensive sauvignon blanc from the presidential bar. I needed to be as calm and focused as I'd ever been, but that was a big order, as I knew we could end up dead, disgraced, or dying in a Vietnamese jail. This was not a movie, not a tourism commercial. This was taking a big chance. And here I was, back in a place I never wanted to be.

I could walk away. Hanoi's airport was an hour away, but I had a deep loyalty to Bao and his men, who had been killed and wounded trying to protect us. I also felt a real love for Nachi, but my feelings were so confused that I had little confidence in where I stood.

On one level, I admired her for thinking of a very original way to bring the Hoi An Massacre to the world. She was on the cover of the Asian edition of People magazine, for crying out loud. It had a big photo of her at the podium in The Nam Hai ballroom after she'd been released, looking like the most beautiful bald woman in the world.

On the other hand, I hated her for using me as a chess piece, for lying the whole time, and for setting in motion all these events that got all these people killed. I tried to put my anger in a box and focus on the moment.

CHAPTER *4 2*

At five in the morning I handed An Dung, the head of security, the Oshima American Express Platinum Card —our *blank check*— and a half hour later, he returned with $50,000 US dollars inside a black plastic bag. I had no idea how he did it; the banks were closed, and it was a little too much cash for an ATM. But I just signed a slip, and that was it.

I could hear Nachi and Hai getting ready, taking showers, and drying their hair. Nachi came out looking like a totally different person, in a short black wig and wearing a surgical mask.

"What do you think?"

"I wouldn't know it's you."

Surgical masks were a common sight in Hanoi. I had seen thousands of people wearing them on their motorbikes because of the intense air pollution that would invade the city. Many women also wore them to protect their skin from the sun so that they wouldn't look like sunburned peasant fieldworkers.

Bao and two of his detectives joined us for breakfast, and we reviewed the plan and the timing of the events. We left the suite and were escorted into the elevator and down to the Mistress Tunnel. Two of Bao's other men had left ahead of us.

When we walked out of the building, it was an unusually clear day. No pollution, a deep-blue sky, with the temperature in the seventies. We walked across the park under the dappled shade of the giant elm trees and into the Old Quarter.

There was an immense amount of energy and activity on the treelined street that we were going to block off. One lane was already shut down, and a dozen production assistants were laying down the dolly tracks. Another group was unloading a big white semitrailer and slowly backing a camera dolly down a ramp. A generator truck was quietly running as the electrical people erected big banks of theatrical lights.

Hanoi had many dragon-dance troupes, and by the looks of things, we had three of the best. The dragons were predominantly yellow, with red trim and huge, fierce-looking dragon heads. All of them were held aloft on long poles by the dragon dancers who were dressed in impeccable yellow and red silk costumes with bright green sashes tied around their waists.

The dancers practiced their up and down movements, which made the dragons undulate like sixty-foot snakes. One of the dragons had a rig that produced puffs of smoke from its nostrils. Simultaneously, six drumming teams began warming up on big kettle drums on wheels that would follow the dragons, which gave it an instant excitement like the start of a college football game.

To get everyone in the mood for the performance, one of the pyrotechnic guys set off a very loud M-80 firecracker, which sounded just like a hand grenade. With the big camera mounted on the dolly, the shooting crew practiced running it up and down the track, making sure they had it uniformly level and free from bumps that could jar the camera. GoPro cameras were also mounted on the dragons themselves to get a dragon's point of view as the dancers weaved in and out through the crowds and down the street.

A couple hours later, Quoc Huy delivered on his promise to supply the extras. But instead of three hundred people, there were well over five hundred and more kept coming. Soon we had the five-way intersection and two full blocks of the street lined with people three deep the whole way. It was a perfect scene with hundreds of happy extras. Little kids, old men, lovely women—they all looked like they were having a good time.

Someone gave me a bullhorn, and I gave it to Hai, "Tell them that we want to go three dragons abreast, with the center dragon about twenty yards ahead of the other two. When we go into the intersection, I want them to form a conga line and circle the intersection and keep doing it." He nodded at me, and suddenly his voice was booming out of the bullhorn in Vietnamese.

I don't know exactly what he said, but everyone seemed to understand. There were no confused looks from the dancers. Everyone checked in on walkie-talkies, and we were ready to go. I yelled, "Action," over the bullhorn, and it all began—intense drumming and exploding strings of firecrackers, with the yellow satin dragons coming fully alive.

At the same time, two Hanoi Gas Company technicians were going door to door, checking for gas leaks that had been reported in the area. One carried a portable gas detector that pulled samples from ground level. The other carried a canvas satchel for tools.

They went into shops, knocked on apartment doors, and even stopped people on the street to ask if anyone had smelled a gas leak. Eventually, they started working their way down the alley that led to Truong Van's house.

The shoot was going like clockwork. The dragons broke into formations that I hadn't asked for, but it looked terrific as they went swirling around, moving down the street.

As the first dragon entered the intersection, the crowd grew louder. The pyrotechnic guys set off more M-80s and dozens of strings of smaller firecrackers. Riding on the camera dolly, I looked up and saw Truong Van with his entourage of bodyguards watching from a nearby second-story balcony. I had the cameraman tilt up and take their picture.

The dragons circled the intersection five or six times and that was all the footage we needed. Hai invited all the extras and onlookers to join us in the middle of the street, and the neighborhood party began. Craft service went through the crowd and gave out fruit drinks, coconut water, pork buns, and chicken wings.

I cracked open a magnum bottle of Veuve Clicquot champagne and held it up as a toast to Truong Van and his guards. I asked Hai to get on the bullhorn and invite them to come down and join us. The drummers kept playing, and the dragons kept dancing.

The crowd parted as Truong Van, Quoc Huy, and his men moved toward us. We greeted them with glasses of champagne. The guards stayed stone-faced.

"Thank you for your help," I said in Vietnamese, like Hai had coached me, and handed Truong Van the $50,000 in the black bag. He had a thin mustache and a neutral expression, and he was wearing what looked like English bench-made shoes.

At that exact time, the Hanoi Gas Company technicians approached the single ponytailed guard at the entrance to the white house. They told him about all the reports of gas leaks in the neighborhood and that they needed to check inside the house. The guard looked closely at their photo-ID badges, turned, and unlocked the front door. He led them down a narrow, winding stairway to the basement. It had a strong musty smell and was packed with video-gambling games, mainly electronic slot machines.

The technicians turned on the gas detector and slowly began a tour of the different storage rooms. The guard stayed with them for five minutes and then went back upstairs. The technicians then found the boiler room behind a steel door at the far end of the basement. From their satchel, they removed a forged wrench and a foot-long propane cylinder that was strapped with half a stick of dynamite, a battery, and an electronic cell-phone-triggering device. It was all held together with duct tape.

They then used the wrench to open the gas line where it entered the building. It made a strong hissing sound. They quickly left the room but were very careful when they closed the steel door so as not to generate a spark.

Back outside, they told the guard that everything seemed to be all right and started walking down the alley toward the intersection where the street party was still going on.

Truong Van and his entourage of bodyguards were walking the other way. They were laughing and looking inside the bag at the $50,000. The gas company technicians stopped to let them pass and watched them walk down the alley to the front door of his white house. Truong Van spoke to the ponytail guy at the door and went inside, followed by his men.

With that, one of the technicians pulled out a cell phone, punched in ten numbers, and hit "send." It was as if the whole building came off the foundation; all the windows on all three stories were blown out at once, and the single building collapsed sending out a cloud of white dust and orange flames. People were screaming, running, and hitting the ground next to a flattened yellow dragon. Complete confusion. Total pandemonium.

The Hanoi Gas Company technicians, Bao's two detectives, walked slowly through the crowd that was pushing in to see what had happened.

CHAPTER 43

One by one, we all returned to the office building as the sounds of sirens echoed throughout the city. We met in the basement. There were no smiles, no celebration. The Metropole guard unlocked the door to the Mistress Tunnel, and we walked the two blocks back to the hotel and took the private elevator up to the Imperial Suite.

An Dung was waiting for us at the door. Inside, his security people had created a Buddhist shrine to the dead, using a credenza in the living room as an altar with four framed black-and-white photos of the four officers who had been killed by the IED in Da Nang. Each photo was draped with a black ribbon in front of a silver incense burner with smoke curling into the air. We kneeled before the altar, all eight of us, and prayed for their souls, as a gong was rung four times.

At that very moment, I could see the faces of all the people I'd killed in my life. They silently passed before my eyes—dozens of NVA and Vietcong soldiers, their bodies being dragged out of buildings, their eyes open, and their young faces twisted in horror. I saw all the civilians we had accidently killed in the crossfire— old men, women, and children—filling me with a breathtaking sadness.

I even saw the faces of the brutal thugs we had just blown off the face of the Earth, less than an hour earlier. In my heart, I apologized to them all, even though so many of them had been doing everything in their power to kill me and my people. I prayed for forgiveness.

We finally got up and looked at each other. Bao lit a cigarette. Nachi took off her wig. Hai called his wife on his cell phone. I shook hands with the detectives who had played the gas company technicians and the two who had been with us. Nobody smiled.

I felt as drained as I'd ever felt in my life as I flashed back to going through an intersection in Hue where some Vietnamese ARVN troops had been in a ghastly fight. They'd been eating rations, and twenty NVA bodies had been piled up before them on the sidewalk. The stench was overwhelming. It was like death was entering your body through your nostrils, forever corrupting your soul, killing your spirit.

CHAPTER *44*

Shortly thereafter, we started packing up. Nachi had us booked on a Japan Airlines 787 flight to Tokyo. Before we left, we again kneeled before the four photos of the dead Hoi An police officers. Bao spoke to the photos in Vietnamese as if those men were in the room, saying that we had avenged their deaths and the people who had killed them were no more. He told them not to worry; their families in Hoi An would be taken care of, and they would be remembered as heroes.

The gong sounded four more times. The eight of us made a pact that we would take the secret of what we had done to the grave.

Bao said, "The money, the orders, the yakuza mafia guys with five million dollars—all of it came from

Japan. We will not honor these officers until we find out who is behind it all."

As a bellman was taking our bags out of the room, Hai said, "Look at this."

He had the TV tuned to a local news channel with captions in English. The picture was coming live from the Old Quarter.

A stand-up reporter said in Vietnamese, "Hanoi Gas Company executives have speculated that the explosion of a house in the Old Quarter may have been the result of rusted gas lines that have plagued the aging infrastructure of the Old Quarter for years. Earlier in the day, residents and shop owners were visited by gas company workers who were searching for gas leaks in the area.

"It has been reported that as many as twelve individuals died inside the house explosion, pending final identifications through dental records. The explosion also blew out over a hundred windows in nearby buildings—but no one else was injured as many of the town's residents were participating in a Dragon Dance festival several blocks from the blast.

"We have received confirmation that the house

belonged to a well-known organized-crime figure, who had major interests in bars and restaurants in the Old Quarter. As you can see, fire crews are still on the scene putting out remaining hot spots."

We filed into the elevator and got off in the private lobby; our footsteps echoed off the stone walls. The hotel had a blacked-out stretch van parked on the sidewalk in front of the Opera Wing's side door. We loaded in, the door slid shut, and we were moving. We drove past the Metropole's main entrance and headed for the airport.

I was sitting on the second-row bench seat next to Nachi. She reached over and held my hand. She held it all the way to the airport. We both looked out our windows; a long bridge over the Red River went by. It was like an ineffable understanding passed between us, through our hands. I could feel it inside me, falling into place. I finally knew how I felt about her.

A t Nội Bài International Airport, we were taken through surging crowds of Vietnamese travelers—big families, young couples, and lots of new-looking luggage. Most everyone looked prosperous and excited. Bao showed his badge at the security checkpoint, and we were directed to a line for pilots and aircrews. No metal detectors, no pat down. They just waved us along.

At the gate, Bao and his men were taken to a room behind the ticketing podium, where they gave up their guns and ammunition to a couple of airline stewards. When we got in our seats, I prayed to leave Vietnam completely behind me—all the pain, all the horrible dreams, all the searing memories.

We taxied out to the main runway, and then the

787 came to a halt and started turning around—the giant right engine screaming to make the rotation. The captain came on and announced that a passenger in coach was having heart problems and that we would be returning to the gate. It was the kind of thing that filled me with foreboding that something else was going on. I imagined cops coming on board and arresting all of us.

Instead a medical crew came aboard and worked for a good half hour before taking the passenger off the plane on a stretcher.

We finally pushed away from the gate and took off into the night, with a last flash of Hanoi's skyscrapers streaming by the plane's windows. Wearing her short black wig, Nachi was sitting across the aisle from me. I watched her reading a Japanese paperback in the cone of yellow light from her reading lamp. She had taken off her surgical mask and was drinking a glass of white wine; she looked serene.

Bao sat next to me on the flight and told me about his colleague, an old-timer cop with the Tokyo Metropolitan Police who had managed to stay clean despite the daily presence of police corruption all around him. "He said that they are a hundred times worse than our petty Vietnamese police who shake down cab drivers. These guys are into drugs, prostitution, money laundering, beating confessions out of defendants and destroying evidence—and that's just for starters."

The guy told Bao that the biggest organized criminals in Japan were actually their own national police force. He said that there were factions of the police suspected of consorting with the yakuza. It's part of the reason why the yakuza are not outlawed in Japan; they are actually regulated and monitored. And while the majority of their money-making is illegal, some also run legit businesses—that's why they have offices, business cards and operate in public. The twenty-two yakuza clans rake in over $80 billion dollars a year. If they were rated like a normal business, they would be considered Japan's second largest private equity group.

Plus, the Japanese laws had also been designed to make it very difficult for a yakuza police investigation to go after the top guys. There was no plea-bargaining, so there was no incentive for low-ranking yakuza to talk for a lighter sentence. There was rarely wiretapping and no witness-protection program. No undercover work was allowed, and there was no witness relocation either. So they could threaten whole families and kill anyone who would testify against them.

And when the yakuza aren't out competing with the police for protection money from everyone in sight, they did unexpected things like be the first organization to form a rescue team to bring convoys of aid to the tens of thousands affected by the Fukushima disaster. They even had a helicopter bring in food and medicine while evacuating the seriously injured. The government was woefully slow in acting, but not the yakuza. They poured on the aid, without being asked. The corrupt cops and the valiant gangsters—it was like some ancient Japanese Kabuki play with lots of guns and money.

Most amazing of all was that the yakuza were deeply involved with Tokyo Energy and Power's nuclear program. This included blackmail, extortion, construction, real-estate collections, financial-market manipulation, and protection rackets.

The yakuza would also supply the workers—"the marginalized, outcasts"—to do the dangerous nuclear work no one else would do. They were called the "Walking Dead."

CHAPTER **46**

Tokyo itself has the largest metropolitan police force in the world, with over forty thousand officers, plus staff and part-time police on top of that. Your basic standing army. But as far as we were concerned, there was only one man in the Tokyo Metropolitan Police Force we had reason to trust. He was a deputy inspector, named Hitoshi Ozawa, with the Organized Crime Task Force. He was the guy who had warned Bao about the yakuza assassins that had flown to Da Nang. If he hadn't called, we'd all be dead. He had also arranged to get international-police credentials that allowed Bao and his men to carry guns in Japan.

We landed four hours later at Narita International. We went through customs in the aircrew line where Bao and his guys got their guns back. Nachi had three dark-gray Lexus sedans waiting to take us to the Mandarin Oriental—located in Tokyo's Nihonbashi Mitsui Tower.

It was rainy and dark. The outrageous Tokyo video billboards and neon signs blurred the rain into a wash of colors that surrounded the car with a bright, constantly moving tapestry, as soft Japanese rock and roll purred from the radio. Bao told the lead driver that we wanted to drive by Oshima's headquarters.

We rode for fifteen minutes, and there it was—this huge fifty-two-story, green-glass mirrored building. It was lit with searchlights, and the corners of the structure came together to form a vertical sword blade on each end of the office tower. Even though it was less than ten years old, the building had a dark history.

Oshima had hired the very best architects and structural engineers. But when the building had been completed and six thousand employees had moved in, it was discovered that the building would sway twenty-five feet at the top during high winds. In the executive offices on the fiftieth floor, people were complaining about motion sickness and the disconcerting sight of plant baskets attached to the ceiling, swaying back and forth in a wide arc.

The engineers were brought back in and shown the seriousness of the problem. They proceeded to run wind-tunnel tests on a scale model of the Oshima building. When they simulated an eighty-mile-per-hour wind coming from the west/southwest, the building twisted and collapsed. With the right wind coming from the right direction, six thousand employees could die.

Being Japanese, being Oshima, they kept it a secret. But they became very interested in the weather. They also began an all-out campaign to find a solution, without others finding out how bad the situation was.

Huge crews worked at night installing a counterweight of five hundred thousand pounds on the top floor, which was connected to the four corners of the building by giant springs. The massive lead counterweight sat on an oiled steel plate, which was connected to the springs. The counterweight provided a powerful force for resisting the corners being pushed out of position in the high wind.

Oshima had kept the secret from the thousands of Oshima employees—lives that had been put at risk for well over a year—while the fix was being made. That's until one of the structural engineers decided to write a book.

In fact, Oshima had tried to stop it from being published. But by then, no one cared, and the news outlets did not want to promote the discovery and embarrass Oshima—their biggest buyer of advertising time and space.

CHAPTER *47*

When we got to the Mandarin Oriental, we were taken to the lobby on the thirty-eighth floor. We walked out of the elevator to a stupendous, panoramic view of Tokyo's skyline at night, with three-story-high windows all framed in dark wood showcasing the view. Checking us in were two Japanese girls dressed in matching yellow-silk kimonos, who seemed to know as many languages as Nachi, including the body-language part. Cute, smart, friendly. Keeping track of the eight electronic room keys and the booking arrangements, they escorted us to our rooms.

Bao had a corner suite, so once we had all dropped off our luggage in our rooms, we headed down to his place. He was standing in front of an L-shaped leather couch with another stunning view of the Tokyo skyline glowing behind him. He had his jacket off with a black Glock automatic in a shoulder holster resting under his left arm. He was drinking a glass of red wine and watching the local news. We sat down on the couch, and Bao lit up a cigarette and began talking to us as he paced around the room.

"As you know, we are very interested in finding out who gave the yakuza five million dollars to kill Nachi and everyone involved with her abduction. For this reason, I have brought in a team of elite hackers I know and trust. They're two guys I originally arrested for hacking into the Hoi An police database. At the time, they were students trying to find out if the police had evidence on a friend who had been arrested after a bar fight.

"They found out their friend was okay, but the Hoi An police tracked them down for hacking into our system. We gave them a choice: go to jail or work for us at full pay. We have done several investigations with them, and I have yet to see a computer system they could not break into. Currently they are working on the network of the Hamaguma, the largest yakuza syndicate in the country with over fifty thousand members. It's based in Kobe but has a strong presence here in Tokyo. My guys know a hundred ways to break into a network from brute-force attacks to Trojan-horse deceptions, where they assume the identity of a trusted ally.

The cigarette smoke swirled around his head, and followed him as he paced the room. "They know how to create back doors to systems and how to con system administrators into giving out passwords, by making them think that they're talking to supervisors in the same company. If there is a trail of money or correspondence, they will find it. They are also very good at not leaving any tracks."

A half hour later, Deputy Inspector Hitoshi Ozawa showed up at Bao's suite and was ushered into the living room. He was a stocky, middle-aged man wearing a dated three-piece suit. He presented his business card to each of us with two hands and followed it up with plenty of bowing.

Oddly, he spoke English with an American southern accent that made him sound like he'd learned it from someone in Georgia. He told us about the yakuza's large-scale corporate-bribery program called *Sokaiya*. "It goes like this: the yakuza buy enough shares in a company to guarantee them a place at the annual shareholders meeting. Next they dig up as much dirt as possible on the company's leadership—things like adultery, alcoholism, drug use, or shady financial dealings. Then they very politely tell the company's leaders, 'Give us money, or we will come to the shareholders meeting and embarrass you.' Since we Japanese fear shame above nearly everything, this tactic has worked thousands of times.

"It's why ninety percent of the companies on the Tokyo Stock Exchange have their annual meetings on the same day; it's based on the theory that the yakuza can't be everywhere at once," he shrugged his shoulders. "At the same time, many corporations employ the yakuza for extralegal jobs nobody else wants to go near, like the "Walking Dead" going into the Fukushima disaster and covering their radiation badges with lead so that they wouldn't show the huge amounts of radiation they were getting from working on the reactors."

He continued. "The result of all this is that the yakuza, the police, the government, and the corporations are all tied together in a massive criminal enterprise that very few people want to change. And the ones who do are powerless."

CHAPTER *48*

After the deputy inspector left, I knew we had to tell Bao the whole story. I had no idea how he'd react, but we couldn't leave him in the dark any longer. It was too dangerous. I talked with Nachi and Hai, and they both agreed that it was time. We met with Bao after his detectives had gone to their rooms. We all sat on the L-shaped leather couch. Bao and Nachi sat on one side; Hai and I sat on the other.

Nachi started, "I should be the one to tell you that there is more about Hoi An and that I have lied to you."

"And now you are going to tell me?" Bao asked.

"Yes. We thought it best to keep it a secret." She paused, exhaling a deep breath. "But the truth is that my abduction was staged by a secret production arm of Oshima Advertising. The kidnapping was acted out. The two students played my abductors, and the old man who committed hara-kiri was an actor in a special-effects studio in Tokyo.

"Absolutely everything we said about the Hoi An Massacre is true," she continued. "My grandfather's confession was taken word for word from his diary, as were the pictures of the Hoi An women being shot and children being beheaded. We thought it was the only way that we could get the attention of the world and get the Japanese to apologize for something they have always lied about."

It was as if Bao already knew. He nodded like she had just told him the weather report for the next day.

"But," she said, "There is more. We saw on the news that Hiro Toma, the creative director I worked with on our deception project, drowned while diving on the Great Barrier Reef. We think he was murdered, along with a technician in the special-effects studio at Oshima, who fell off a balcony here in Tokyo. You already know about the two students I worked with who were tortured and killed."

Looking directly at Nachi, Bao calmly lit another

cigarette and concluded, "So someone is trying to kill everyone on the project, using the yakuza to do it."

He immediately got on his phone and called his hackers in Hoi An. He spoke to them in Vietnamese. Hai told me that he instructed them to turn their attention to Oshima itself—that they were looking for a secret group that had hired the Hamaguma assassins. He told them to give Hiro Toma's e-mails special attention.

I felt hugely embarrassed that we hadn't told Bao the whole story earlier. "I am sorry. When Nachi told us that it was a staged abduction, we thought it would be a disaster if the truth came out. That the Hoi An Massacre would be discredited and ignored all over again."

Bao said, "We have all been puppets in this story." Bao's calmness made it worse. No one said anything for a long time. I felt stupid and small for not having shown him Hiro Toma's business card when I had picked it up out of the grass at the farm.

Bao quizzed us about our connections at Oshima for the Vietnam project. We told him about the British creative team we worked with—Reg Blair and Colin Taylor.

Nachi said, "I don't think they know anything.

They gave us our marching orders as to the scope of the project, the hotels, and the cities to be shot. Our deception was an overlay on their shoot. We'd worked with them before, and their only interest was in doing a top-notch job."

Bao urged, "I think you should go and see them tomorrow."

"We could do that," I said. "If we're going to play this out, we've got to show them the footage, give them a report on the shoot, and get the editing going."

Nachi called and left a message that we were in Tokyo and that we'd like to come over and see them.

CHAPTER **49**

e ended up going over the next afternoon without Nachi. We got out of the cab in front of Oshima's looming headquarters.

I looked at Hai and asked him, "Are you rolling?"

"Oh, yeah, I've been rolling since we left the Mandarin."

We entered the huge marble-clad lobby with a lighted-yellow ceiling and went straight up to the guard desk where we told them our names and whom we were visiting. They handed us visitor name tags and told us someone would come down to escort us upstairs. Hundreds of ponytailed young creatives wearing skinny jeans and account executives in immaculate designer suits were streaming in and out of the building. Everyone coming in had their security badges checked. Ten minutes later Reg Blair appeared in the lobby. He had salt-and-pepper hair and was dressed in blue jeans, soft Italian-leather loafers, and a $3,000 Zegna sport coat.

He stuck out his hand and said, "Well, isn't this wonderful. We were so worried about the three of you. It was all over the news for days and days. Absolutely changing things here, new government and all that. Is Nachi all right?"

"She's okay," I said, "but she's got a touch of the flu. She's resting, but in the meantime, we'd like to show you some of the rough footage. Wait until you see the amazing scenes we shot in Hanoi."

We went up in the elevator to the fortieth floor, walked out into the hall and through glass doors etched in English and in Japanese with the words "Oshima Creative Force."

In the lobby, there were forty-some people who clapped and cheered as we walked by. Colin Taylor stepped forward, shook our hands, and gave us pats on the back.

"You made it. We all want to welcome you back."

"You're not going to believe it," I said. "Despite all our problems, we got pretty much all the shots we were going for, except Ha Long Bay."

"Well, come this way," he said. "We can't wait to see what you've got."

The crowd dispersed; people went back to their offices and workstations as we went down the hall to an editing suite. Hai pulled out his laptop along with two big hard drives and handed them over to the editor. Hai sat next to him at the console as the editor plugged in the hard drives and typed in the password to activate the editing computer. The first thing that came up was the footage from Hue.

We had some forty hours of images, but Hai had it organized in a highlight reel to give Colin and Reg an idea of the types of shots we captured. Right away they were liking the footage from Ho Chi Minh City and the Park Hyatt Saigon and the night shots we had taken before Hai had been hit by the van.

The three of us—Reg, Colin, and I—sat at a second console behind Hai and the editor. It went on for hours. Coffee, tea, sandwiches, and sushi were brought in. The days and weeks rolled by on the big HD screen. We had some excellent shots of riding in a limo up to the former French governor's home in Hue. It had been restored into a luxury boutique hotel, La Residence Hotel and Spa, which seemed right out of a Humphrey Bogart movie. Sitting on the banks of the Perfume River and overlooking the former Imperial Citadel, it had countless 1930s art-deco details, representing the glory days of that period. We turned the footage into black and white, with strong silver highlights. It looked very glamorous for a first pass.

After five hours, we had a pretty good sample to show to the account people and Oshima upper management. The editor typed in a password and logged onto the agency's e-mail. He sent the video link to something like thirty people. The editor went down lists of e-mail addresses on the screen and clicked away.

Reg and Colin were happy and animated as they talked about what a good campaign it was going to be. Hai and I rode back in a cab to the Mandarin. Quietly I asked him, "How did it go?"

He tapped the GoPro button camera under his sport coat. "I got four passwords, which we can read when we slow down the footage of the guy typing them in. I also have about three hundred e-mail addresses, which we can freeze and copy."

CHAPTER 50

At about half past ten that evening, there was a knock at my door. I looked through the eyepiece and saw a round fish-eye image of Nachi standing in the hall, wearing a white robe and slippers.

I opened the door, and she asked, "Can I sleep with you tonight?"

I was half-awake and very slow on the uptake. "Sure. Come on in."

She looked me in the eye as I closed the door. "Christian, I do not want sex. I just want to hear you breathing and know that I'm not alone. I've never had anyone want to kill me before. I need to be with you."

We walked into the bedroom. I pulled back the

covers on the bed. She took off her robe and draped it over an armchair. She was wearing oversized navy-blue and white-striped cotton pajamas, buttoned all the way to her neck—with her unbelievable body underneath. Fluffing up the pillow, she got in on the near side of the bed and I covered her up and tucked her in. I shut off the lights and left only the gleaming Tokyo skyline to dimly illuminate the room as I got into bed with her—our shoulders touching.

She asked me, "Christian, when was the first time you felt unconditionally loved?"

"That's a good question ... It was definitely by my grandfather, Leonard Lindstrom. He was a seventy-year-old wheat farmer. I think I got my whole idea of love from him. Every summer, starting at age five, I was shipped off to his farm on a Trailways bus that stopped at every small town between Kansas City and Courtland, Kansas. My grandmother, Daisy, was in the first stages of Alzheimer's, which made her stern, grumpy, and a little bit scary. She worked around the farmhouse and would hum tunelessly.

"But my grandfather, Leonard, was a completely different story, especially as I came from a home where my parents were unhappy most of the time. He was a tall, handsome Swede who'd been a star football player in college and was still in perfect shape. He'd wear a white shirt and bib overalls and towered over me. From the moment I got to the farm, it was like magic—all the animals, the big machines, and the barns to explore. He had a quiet warmth and a friendliness that I had never experienced in my life. He bought me a brand-new Daisy air rifle and enough canisters of BBs to start a small war. I was five, and I was armed.

"He insisted that I drive the pickup truck around a pasture even when my feet could barely touch the pedals, and I couldn't see over the steering wheel. Every time I'd let out the clutch, the old Ford would jerk and buck, and he'd just say, 'You're doing fine. Give it some more gas.'

"I was crushed when he died, and I had to go from the farm to a sad, hostile home where no one had an ounce of joy."

I paused and then asked, "When was the first time you felt it?"

"Well, my parents were sweet. I was their prize. They convinced me that I was a princess because I'd learned to talk. I had a crown and a fairy outfit, and

I'd walk around and tell them what to do, which they politely ignored. My dad died years ago, but I still feel such love from my mom. She has a great heart, but finding out that my grandfather, who lived in our house, was a mass murderer deeply affected her. Every day she would burn incense and pray for the people who had died."

CHAPTER *51*

I was intoxicated just being in the same room with her and hearing her breathe. I drifted off. When I awoke in the morning, she was gone.

After breakfast, Hai and I had a giant brain dump with Bao on the passwords, the e-mails, and the lead on Arashi Tojo, Nachi's old boyfriend and boss. Bao phoned it all in to his hackers in Hoi An.

The hackers reported they'd discovered e-mails going from a Kobe yakuza office to Oshima and that Hiro Toma's computer had been wiped clean. They said they were working to find his e-mails on a backup server. They thought the passwords that we'd given them might help them break into the next layer of the Oshima computer network. Bao told them to also do a complete Internet search on Arashi Tojo, from the day he was born to his entire career at the agency—bank records, charge cards, everything.

Interestingly enough, they had also discovered the fact that the deposed Japanese prime minister had begun his career as an Oshima account executive. That's right, an Oshima account executive.

Hai and I were scheduled to go over to Oshima to work on the edit at eleven. The morning papers were filled with news of the campaigns for the next prime minister's job. The Liberal Democratic Party, the New Komeito Party, and the Democratic Party of Japan were all working to rally support by winning campaigns in the House of Representatives, which had the ultimate say as to who would become the new prime minister. The Liberal Democratic Party, despite the name, was very conservative and had been the dominant party for years. It was the party of the corporations. There were also tiny parties with little power, like the Happiness Realization Party.

Hai said, "You just can't make this stuff up."

Unlike previous national elections, which were usually focused on the economy, in this one, the subject of the Pacific War atrocities was front and center. All candidates seemed to be saying the same thing. One of them was on an English-speaking news channel.

The candidate said, "The only way Japan can put the Pacific War behind us is to acknowledge the widespread campaign of genocide and slavery that we visited upon our neighbors. It was our campaign of terror and conquest, which we have minimized and denied, while our neighbors and trading partners are painfully aware of the twenty million people we killed in their countries. Facing the past honestly and atoning for our crimes will allow us to move forward with greater harmony."

Hai and I rode over to Oshima in a taxi. I kept thinking about Nachi's question about where love comes from. I could see my wife's face, forever twenty-eight, and the two marines who had literally laid down their lives for me. It was what I felt for Nachi. I loved every second I was with her, whether she was being honest with me or not. I thought she was, but on another level, I didn't care. I was that far gone.

CHAPTER *52*

The next day, Nachi set up a call with a freelance producer who had been shooting movies in Tokyo for years and had an encyclopedic knowledge of the dark side of Tokyo. Her name was Yoshie Kimura.

We explained that we were writing and casting a movie about the Japanese underworld and we needed to meet an expert on the yakuza to give us more of a historical background. She was unfazed by the request and told us she'd get back to us.

We went down to Bao's room, where he had his men planning to put a tail on Arashi Tojo, the "Mr. Fix It" guy. It was not an easy task, as the Oshima building and parking garage had a high level of security. It wasn't as if they could wander around the parking areas looking for a black Audi A8, with a five-digit plate number. But they did know where he was living: the new Aman Tokyo, a stunningly beautiful five-star luxury hotel high in the sky, like the Mandarin Oriental.

There, the staff literally interviewed every person they didn't know before they'd let them enter the elevator going up to the private thirty-third-floor lobby. If you were not a guest or didn't have permission of a guest, they very politely would not let you in. And even if you were invited by a guest, they would personally escort you to your destination. Whether it was the bar or someone's room, they went with you the whole way. It was all done with a smile and lighthearted charm, but no one was getting near the private apartment Arashi Tojo had on the thirty-seventh floor.

The only solution was to put men a block away on the streets that fed the motor entrance and exit. Bao assigned his guys to sit in taxi cabs near the Aman, waiting for someone who would never show up.

After we'd had a room-service lunch, Yoshie Kimura called back to say she had lined up an interview with Mr. Shintaro Yazawa, the man who had run the most famous night club in Asia for over thirty years:

the New Latin Quarter, in Tokyo's Akasaka district.

Fashioning his club after New York City's Latin Quarter nightclub, Mr. Yazawa had played host to most of the top performers in the world, like Nat King Cole, Tony Bennett, Ray Charles, Sammy Davis Jr., Louis Armstrong, the Platters, Ella Fitzgerald, the Supremes, B. B. King, Dolly Parton, Tom Jones, and Barry Manilow. He had brought Western entertainment to Japan for the first time.

At the same time, the club had been patronized by a legion of spies from the CIA, MI-6, and the KGB, and by godfathers from competing yakuza families. It was all common knowledge, as he had written a popular book about his experiences with the club.

He had proved himself a master diplomat and had provided his guests with one hundred of the most gorgeous hostesses in all of Japan—if you were lucky enough to sit at one of the club's eighty tables.

We met him in the lobby of the Mandarin. I had heard he was eighty years old, but standing in front of me was a dapper gentleman in an impeccable blue suit and red tie, with a snap-brim straw hat and lightness in his step like a latter-day Fred Astaire.

We shook hands. Yoshie introduced each of us in Japanese, and we took the elevator to Bao's suite. Before we sat down, he did the Japanese two-handed presentation of his business card. I did the same, both of us bowing our heads. He asked in Japanese, "What would you like to know?"

I said, "The history of the yakuza and the name of the person in power now."

He spoke in Japanese for several minutes, and Yoshie translated.

"The first thing you must understand," he said, "is that the yakuza is as old as Japan itself. A thousand times older than our democracy. It originally started as an organization that provided protection from bandits and the ravages of feudal Japan.

"The New Latin Quarter was bankrolled by my benefactor, Mr. Kodama, who was a high-powered political fixer in Japan. He had the crazy idea that I could run the club, even though I was only twenty-six.

"We started recruiting top musical talent from the States. The club took off. It was packed every night. Powerful people made reservations weeks, months in advance, just to get in.

"It was also something of a balancing act. The spies were after the hostesses, and the yakuza dons didn't want a table near another family. Every night was a stage play.

"You see, this was totally new for Japan. In the old days, the cabaret men would come for the hostesses, who would entertain them by lighting their cigarettes, pouring drinks, flirting, and dancing with them. Modern-day geishas of sorts. Sometimes the men would get attached to a hostess, and if she left, they would follow her to another club. We called it 'Water Business' because it flowed away."

Everyone laughed.

"It was Mr. Kodama's idea to bring in the entertainment," he continued. "Through his connections with the American military, he had access to the American talent coming to entertain the US troops. After they performed on the base, he would pay them a lot of money to come play at the club the next night.

"So this is my book, *Undenied*," he said, handing me a volume with a picture of the New Latin Quarter on the cover. "And it has a chart that explains the relationship of the people involved and the connection to Mr. Kodama."

"How did Mr. Kodama get so powerful?" I asked.

"Many years ago, the Japanese government contracted him to help move supplies out of China in order to help the Japanese war effort. He collected ammunitions and raw materials necessary for the war. He became part of a very, very important outsourcing organization for the Japanese Navy during the wartime. He also got involved in the drug trade and moved opiates to Japan alongside the government supplies he was smuggling in.

"The Japanese Navy stole diamonds, gold, and platinum from Shanghai to pay for the future expense of the war, and then the war ended. Mr. Kodama was responsible for transporting these things.

"When the war was over, the government never asked for them back, so he kept them. That's how he became one of the richest men in Asia. Later he used his power and his money to finance the start of the Liberal Democratic Party."

Nachi asked, "And he was your uncle?"

Mr. Yazawa responded. "Uncle Boss. Mr. Kodama was a very, very important person in Japan. He would do favors, large and small, for people in key places and would collect from them later.

"When the first Latin Quarter started, they made it look like Mr. Kodama was the one who organized it, but it was actually started by the American mafia, a man called Ted Ruin, who stayed behind the scenes. They paid Mr. Kodama's organization to be their front.

"But Ted Ruin had a different purpose for the club—he wanted to run casinos. But the Japanese government didn't like the idea of gambling and casinos. So even though they opened the first Latin Quarter, they couldn't open a casino. But still they did it, only it was kind of a casino that wasn't public."

"Private?" Nachi asked.

"Hidden. So people thought it was just a nightclub, but behind the scenes, it was a working casino.

"Around the same time, an important politician, Aiichiro Fujiyama, then the foreign minister, began building an international-class hotel next to the Latin Quarter, and they needed more land and wanted the club to relocate. But the club was making too much money, and they refused to move. That's when the fire started, accidentally."

The whole room broke out in laughter.

CHAPTER **53**

"So that started the war between the American mafia and the Japanese yakuza," Mr. Yazawa explained. "The American mafia didn't want to move because they were making too much money from the secret casino. But Mr. Kodama wanted to support the Japanese foreign minister. So he told Ted Ruin to leave and return to the United States. And then the fire happened. So the Latin Quarter closed."

I asked, "Did the yakuza set the fire?"

"It's a secret," he said, "and nobody knows. Lots of guessing. I have heard many things. Some people say it was set; some say it was just an accident. I think the fire was set. The Latin Quarter had fire insurance, and Mr. Kodama received a huge amount of money."

"So when they got all that money, is that when they decided to build the New Latin Quarter?" I asked.

"After the fire," said Mr. Yazawa, "Ted Ruin was forced to leave the country. He went to the Philippines but could never come back to Japan."

Bao followed up. "Did the government make him leave or was it the yakuza?"

He smiled and replied, "The government. At Mr. Kodama's suggestion.

"The reason Mr. Kodama was so influential was because he was the behind-the-scenes power of the leading political party, and he was closely connected to Tokyo's criminal underworld."

"Was the Liberal Democratic Party very conservative then, like it is now?" I asked.

"More idealistic than today. Back then, people still did not know what democracy was. It was a new idea being introduced; democracy was a whole new concept to the Japanese people.

"After the war, people had no idea what the future of the country was going to be with this new system, new government, new everything, so they needed new leadership. That is when Mr. Hatoyama became the first prime minister of the newly-formed Liberal Democratic Party."

"So who was becoming rich during this time?" Nachi asked.

"Secretly, number one, Mr. Kodama," said Mr. Yazawa. "After the war, Mr. Kodama was put in prison as a convicted Class A mass murderer for crimes in China. But then he was pardoned. People still don't know why he was released. Maybe an exchange for information or diamonds.

"But some also think it was the intention of General Douglas MacArthur and the US intelligence community to release him in exchange for his aid in fighting communism. He was a big, right-wing ultranationalist with a vast network of contacts, so he would have easily agreed to root out communist sympathizers and fight the socialist presence in Japan at the time. So he got out after three years."

"Which is unusual," I said, "because most of the Class A prisoners were executed."

"Eleven people were executed," he said.

"So he gets out. What does he do? And where is all this money?" I asked.

"That's when he started the Liberal Democratic Party. He never held any prominent political office but was very involved with the leaders of the governing party—many of whom became prime ministers with his help.

"He had a vision for the future of Japan. So when Mr. Hatoyama was chosen to become the first prime minister of the Liberal Democratic Party—knowing that Mr. Kodama was supporting the party and giving them all this money—Mr. Hatoyama asked him, 'Why are you doing this? What is it that you want in return?' Mr. Kodama said there was one thing, and Mr. Hatoyama was ready to hear it, whatever the outcome. And Mr. Kodama said, 'Just protect the emperor.' He was an extreme right-wing nationalist who supported the emperor."

I was beginning to realize that we were up against a very powerful system that had infiltrated every part of Japanese life for generations.

CHAPTER *54*

Looking out of the window, I could see Mount Fuji and a jet flying thousands of feet in the air above it. Mr. Yazawa spoke about the making of Mr. Kodama. "He was born in the north, near Fukushima, and he saw the poverty. The farmers, when they didn't yield a very good crop, had to sell their daughters to the red-light people. Such a miserable life. He saw that the government wasn't helping them at all. This is what he witnessed as a young man.

"Trying to find work, he came to Tokyo. One day the emperor's coach came by, and he gave them a letter for the emperor. It asked for him to help the people in the North."

"That was very brave," Bao said.

"But, of course, the police came and caught him," he explained.

"Did the emperor get the letter?" I inquired.

"They're not sure but probably not. During that time, when the farmers would directly appeal to the emperor, they had to prepare to be killed for that kind of disobedience. So he was ready to accept that very severe punishment. He was actually in prison for two years for doing this. This is how his name became very known," Mr. Yazawa continued.

"Like Robin Hood," I said.

Mr. Yazawa nodded.

"So after the New Latin Quarter got successful, did the yakuza come in and try to take over?" I asked.

"I had Mr. Kodama! Nobody came to bother us. The godfather was behind me."

"So you had no problems?" I asked.

"It was a high-end nightclub. The clients were all the politicians, the imperial family, and the elite. We became the most important representatives, like the Ministry of Foreign Affairs; when they had important guests, they brought them there. Exclusive. The emperor didn't come, but the relatives of the emperor's family came. And all the top members of Japanese industry. Later, everybody would come to know the name of Mr. Kodama. Have you heard about Lockheed?" he asked.

"The Lockheed scandal?" I asked.

"Yes, he was part of it."

"Was he convicted?"

"Yes, but he didn't go to prison," confirmed Mr. Yazawa. "He was confined to house arrest, and then he had the stroke. Many people sympathized with Mr. Kodama's five-million-dollar bribery scandal. He was destroyed. This news was in the newspapers every day. So that's how many more people came to know about Mr. Kodama.

"The Lockheed Aircraft Company was doing business in Japan, trying to sell planes to Japan Airlines. They were told that Mr. Kodama was the most influential person in Tokyo, more so than the prime minister. He used his influence to help them sell planes. He was their secret agent for over ten years."

"One more question about the yakuza," I said.

"I heard this story that when the Fukushima disaster happened and everyone was dying and sick and running out of food, the people who came to the rescue were the yakuza. That they sent convoys of food."

"Oh, yes, it's true," he said. "The Hamaguma. There was also a big earthquake in 1995. At that time, yakuza members went out to help the people, so they went there, rescued people, and cooked rice. They made rice balls for the victims. Then when Fukushima happened, the Hamaguma people went to the rescue there.

"They actually don't like to be called yakuza. The group's motto of Hamaguma is to help people, no matter what people say. The most important thing in their world is *ninkyo*, which means that they are loyal and that they will help the weak people, like Robin Hood. So they like to be called *ninkyo* instead of yakuza, which they hate.

"Because *ninkyo* means good-hearted and loyal— by helping others, helping the weak," he joked, "I am not a member of the Hamaguma."

I laughed, "You're not? I heard you are!"

"That's what the people think," he replied.

"When I look at the situation," I said, "it's like you have these corrupt police and these valiant gangsters who are heroes sometimes. Right?"

He shrugged and said, "But today I must tell you that the real yakuza power is in Kobe," Mr. Yazawa explained. "There is a gentleman there, Mr. Onishi-san, who lives out in the open in a Hamaguma fortress of a house in a wealthy residential neighborhood. He is the don who controls everything. If you are going to shoot a movie about the yakuza, nothing can be done without his permission. He has the power Mr. Kodama once held. I can make some phone calls for you. But whatever you do, go alone."

Mr. Yazawa bowed to us, put on his straw hat, and left.

So there it was. The Liberal Democratic Party, which had been in power for decades, was started with a fortune stolen from China and supplied by the yakuza. A nice foundation for a democracy.

CHAPTER **55**

By then Bao's men had established around-the-clock surveillance of Arashi Tojo— Nachi's old boyfriend and the man we suspected of running the whole deception operation. Bao's detectives had followed him to the Kabukicho red-light district in the Shinjuku area of Tokyo. They'd tailed him to an unattended parking garage, where they Velcroed a GPS broadcasting device underneath his Audi's rear bumper.

As the largest red-light area in Asia, Kabukicho had a powerful sexual energy, with its strip clubs, love hotels, gay bars, and host clubs, where women pay a lot of money for handsome male pampering, joking, dancing, and sometimes just for conversation. The streets seemed to vibrate with the immense flashing lights and gigantic LED video screens from the hundreds of yakuza-owned hostess clubs, the noisy, clanking pachinko parlors, and the hundreds of restaurants and bars.

Bao's men reported that Arashi Tojo had gone to a strip club for several hours, followed by a stop at a hostess club called the Blue Fish, and had made it back to the Aman around three in the morning.

But even better, Bao told us that the hackers had uncovered Arashi Tojo's phone records, which showed hundreds of calls back and forth to Kobe, particularly to a cell tower in the same neighborhood as the Hamaguma fortress, where the *kumichō*, the sixth godfather, resided.

We sat in Bao's suite and listened to the two detectives who had spent the night following Tojo. They passed around an iPhone video of Tojo up on stage with two topless Japanese girls wearing garter belts and high heels. Both girls had outrageous bodies, looking all of sixteen years old. They were singing Billy Joel's "Piano Man," along with a karaoke machine that projected the lyrics and an accompanying instrumental track.

So there he was—this big, pie-faced thug of a man, with two topless girls draped around him, singing into a handheld microphone. What was even more unusual was that he was pretty good, if you can imagine Billy Joel singing with a heavy Japanese accent, along with his birdlike backup singers.

"Sing us a song; you're the piano man. Sing us a song tonight. We're all in the mood for a melody, and you've got us feeling all right."

Nachi thought it was hilarious replaying it several times. She couldn't stop giggling. The two detectives who had followed Tojo around looked like they could fall asleep on the spot.

CHAPTER 56

Several hours later, Nachi knocked on my door with a serious look on her face.

"I just talked to my mother," she said, "and she has been sick for several days. Her doctor thinks she has the flu, which had her seriously dehydrated. She's running a fever, so I'm very worried. I must go see her."

She sat on the bed. I sat on the couch.

"Well," I said, "we're going to have to think about how we can do that. They could still try to kill you. Do they still have police guards on your mother's house?"

"Yes, but since she got sick, they don't come in. They sit outside in a squad car."

We went down to Bao's room. He was on the phone with his people in Hoi An. After twenty minutes, he hung up. Nachi told him about her mother and that she had to go. Bao didn't like letting her leave the safety of the Mandarin.

He finally said, "Okay, but let's do this as carefully as possible. It takes five and a half hours to drive to Kyoto. You've got to go through Yokohama, all down the coast, through Nagoya. It's a long drive and a lot of exposure, being out in the open. If they've got a tail on you, it would not be good."

Nachi said, "If we took the Nozomi bullet train, we'd be there in just over two hours."

"But the first thing," Bao said, "is to get you as unrecognizable as possible."

With the help of a trusted production friend, a movie makeup artist was brought up to the suite to make Nachi look like an eighty-year-old woman. Nachi was given a gray-haired wig, a prosthetic rubber nose, and a sickly tan-and-gray skin color, with crow's-feet and wrinkles across her forehead and around her neck. It was all topped off with a drab housedress and raincoat. She was also given white orthopedic socks and some old-fashioned Geta clogs to wear, which made her shuffle.

She walked around the room a few times like a befuddled old lady.

She said, "I think I need a cane."

I wore a basic, white medical orderly's uniform with a white jacket, a surgical mask, and a white "Tokyo Giants" baseball cap.

Tokyo Station wasn't far from the Mandarin, but with Nachi's slow, feeble walk, we had the hotel car take us there.

The station was a huge complex of traditional buildings that had been rebuilt after the war with large, striking, modern additions. We walked through continuous crowds of travelers, thousands upon thousands trooping by us, trying to avoid running into the old lady. We found our way to where the green train for Kyoto would be stopping. Exactly on time, the sparkling bullet train, with a long green nose and blue trim, entered the station.

The grand-class cabin door snapped open precisely before us, and a beautiful attendant in a high-style stewardess uniform came out and welcomed us aboard. We had large, comfortable, reserved seats, which were identical to what you'd find in business class on an international flight.

After exactly sixty seconds, the train pulled out of the station and smoothly accelerated to over 150 miles per hour. We were flying. The ride was quiet and absolutely smooth. The automatic door at the front of the cabin opened, and another attendant bowed to the carful of passengers and began serving a selection of wines, tea, and other beverages.

Two of Bao's detectives were seated several rows behind us, looking like bored businessmen who didn't know each other. A conductor came through and checked our tickets. But then through the car came a guy with a tattoo peeking out above the edge of his shirt collar and a missing pinky finger on his right hand. He was checking faces, and he might as well have been wearing a sign that screamed "yakuza."

In an instant, the comfortable train ride was over. Instead, I was intensely focused on this guy's hands and eyes as he came down the aisle. I turned my head to the left and saw, at the edge of my vision, Bao's guys getting up. The man was three rows away from us. Bao's men came forward with their cop faces on, and he stopped. As he turned to leave, the detectives went right after him and caught him on the other side of the automatic glass door.

I could see they were bracing him and yelling at him. They eventually let him go. As they passed my seat, one of them said quietly, "He won't be back."

The bullet train rocketed along through miles of rice paddies. For a stretch, we could see Mount Fuji through the afternoon haze. It still had plenty of snow at the top.

Nachi said, "Do you think he picked up on us?"

"We'll see when we get to Kyoto. But I don't think so. He didn't seem to be looking at us."

She said, "Christian, I never thought it would all turn out this way. It's like turning over a rock, and out come the snakes and worms to eat your body."

"I know. This is not going to stop. Unless we can get some leverage on your Tojo guy at Oshima to call off the dogs."

The train blasted through Yokohama. I looked at the eighty-year-old Nachi. She smiled at me, her fake crow's-feet like wings at the corners of her eyes.

The Kyoto train station was a futurist's dream—a light-filled cathedral with fifteen-story glass walls and soaring glass arches. We walked through the giant concourse. Nachi was shuffling along through the crowds, and Bao's men followed about twenty yards back, walking separately, scanning faces. It was dark when we got a cab and rode to Nachi's mother's house. A couple of lights were burning on the second floor, but there were no cops out front.

Nachi fumbled around, looking through her purse to find the house key. We rang the bell. Before Nachi could unlock it, the door opened a crack and then all the way. Standing there was Nachi's sister, Kiki.

Nachi reached out to her and said, "Kiki, where are the police? Where is mother?"

"What happened to you?" Kiki asked, staring at her face.

"It's just makeup. What happened to mother?"

"She got worse. She's been taken to the hospital.

She's in intensive care. I came back to get clothes for her. I am so scared; they had to put her on a ventilator to aid her breathing. It is very bad."

Nachi and Kiki went upstairs to pack a suitcase with everything their mother might need. I stood in the living room where a single spotlight illuminated a painting at the end of the room. At a distance, it looked like Nachi, but as I got closer, I could see it was an older person, Nachi's mother. In the painting, she was standing in front of an incense burner, with the smoke of the incense curling up in the air.

I remembered Nachi telling me that her mother lit incense and prayed every day for the innocent people whom her grandfather had murdered in the three villages outside of Hoi An. I couldn't believe it. Right there in front of me was Nachi's inspiration to make certain that the people killed in the Hoi An Massacre were not forgotten.

They came downstairs with a red suitcase. We locked the house, and Kiki drove us to Kyoto University Hospital. The streets were quiet, the pavement shining from a recent rain.

CHAPTER 58

W e went up to the intensive-care unit on the fourth floor. It was an awful scene. Ruri Tanaka was unconscious, with this big, ugly machine breathing for her; her face was covered by a breathing mask with tubes up her nose and an IV running into the back of her wrist.

When the doctor came in, he said, "It is not the flu. We think she was poisoned."

I looked at Nachi. Even with all the theatrical makeup, I could see that she was shocked. Her mother looked dead. Nachi's shoulders slumped like all her energy had left her body. The best she could do was to stand next to the machines and tubes, holding her mother's lifeless hand, and quietly saying, "I love you, Mother," over and over in Japanese, while Kiki cried inconsolably in the background.

The doctor said that they thought she had been poisoned with a series of small doses of cyanide, enough to make her very sick. For me, it just screamed of the Hamaguma and the woman cop who had been staying in the apartment with Ruri to protect her.

I thought that this was their way of flushing out Nachi and killing her as the last remaining witness to the deception project that had overthrown the government. I was sure the yakuza was Oshima's cleanup crew, making certain there were no loose ends. And they had done it. Nachi was at her mother's bedside, and I had no idea if they were still buying Nachi's disguise.

Bao's detectives stationed themselves in the hall, both on high alert, watching the constant stream of nurses, doctors, technicians, and visitors—all total strangers—passing by her door.

Kyoto University Hospital was a big medical center, with over 1,100 inpatient beds, a staff of 3,000, and an average of 2,900 outpatient visits a day. It was a very busy place. A killer could come from anywhere, carrying flowers.

Several hours later, Bao and his two other detectives

arrived at the hospital after taking the bullet train down from Tokyo. When he came through the door, Bao put a single finger in front of his mouth and then pointed to the ceiling.

I whispered to him, "What do you think?"

"I think we get Nachi out of here. I think the doctors are right." He pointed to Ruri Tanaka, her chest slowly going up and down with the ventilator. "They poisoned her to get Nachi to appear. We've got to assume they're watching this place."

After negotiating with a hospital administrator out in the hall, two orderlies wheeled in a hidden-body gurney, where a cadaver could be lowered below a fake panel in order to make it look like an empty stretcher, making the upsetting scene of a dead body being pushed down the hallway disappear. Nachi didn't want to leave her mother's side. Hugging her sister goodbye, she sobbed as she was led to the gurney. It was an unavoidably creepy scene, watching the crying eighty-year-old Nachi lower herself into the hidden coffin-liken chamber, get covered with the panel, and then wheeled down the hall.

CHAPTER *59*

Nachi was driven in a hospital ambulance to the underground service entrance of the Ritz-Carlton Kyoto, a long, low, four-story luxury hotel on the banks of the Kamogawa River. Like the Mandarin Oriental and the Aman Tokyo, the one-year-old hotel had the most advanced security system I'd ever heard of. Hundreds of cameras all over the hotel were connected to a facial-recognition program that allowed them to keep track of every guest, employee, or outsider who entered the building and their exact real-time locations.

Bao had a long talk with the hotel's chief of security, and we were taken to a large executive suite at the end of the hall on the fourth floor. The curtains were drawn, and the lighting was low. Bao was there waiting for us.

He said, "Our computer people in Hoi An have uncovered evidence of the Hamaguma's collaboration with Mr. Tojo at Oshima. We have a copy of the Oshima money order for the five million in cash, okayed by Tojo. We have e-mails ordering the cleanup of all loose ends. We have text messages. We have phone records. And we still have the two prisoners in Hoi An, who will testify to their role in the assassinations of our officers and the two students.

"Further, I think it's time we contact the *kumichō* in Kobe, Mr. Onishi-san himself, to see if we can find a peaceful understanding between us."

We sat around the low coffee table with the phone in the center. Nachi put it on speakerphone and dialed Yoshie Kimura, the producer and translator who had found Mr. Yazawa.

"Hello, Yoshie. Christian Lindstrom here."

"Oh, yes."

"We would like your help in arranging a call to Mr. Yazawa and translating for us. Could you help us with this?"

"Certainly. I have his number. I'll call you back,"

Yoshie replied.

She called back about an hour later, saying she had arranged a call for eight that evening.

Nachi went into the bathroom and came out twenty minutes later without the makeup, nosepiece, and gray wig. In some ways, she looked worse. Clearly she'd been crying. Her eyes were red and puffy.

We sat on the couch. I put my arm around her, and she started crying uncontrollably, sobbing, her chest heaving.

All I could think to say was, "Let's pray for a miracle."

It was a stupid thing to say, especially as we both knew that her mother looked like she was already gone.

When Yoshie called at eight, Mr. Yazawa was already on the line.

"Hello, Mr. Yazawa-san," I said. "I need your help in getting a message to Mr. Onishi-san."

Yoshie translated, "What is your message?"

"Tell Mr. Onishi-san that I represent the people from Vietnam they have been looking for. I have information that I am certain he will find very valuable. I would like to come see him so that we can negotiate and settle our differences."

Half of me thought I was truly crazy going to see a guy who had been trying to kill us. And we had killed several of his men.

But that was what was actually happening. An hour later Yoshie called back to say that Mr. Yazawa-san had arranged for me to meet with Mr. Onishi-san the following afternoon in Kobe.

Yoshie repeated Mr. Yazawa's last words, "Whatever you do, go alone."

CHAPTER *60*

Kobe was about an hour's drive from Kyoto. If you took the bullet train, it was only a half hour. But we drove in Bao's rental car—a Toyota Crown executive sedan. The car was smooth and quiet, inhaling the superhighway miles. We kept going over what I would say to Mr. Onishi-san, the leader of Japan's largest criminal organization and, for thirty years, untouchable by the police.

I had a thumb drive with a massive amount of information that the Hoi An hackers had uncovered. All of it was illegally obtained, but it could be made useful and legal by telling the police where to look. Hopefully Mr. Onishi-san would be impressed that I had come to him first, and he would not have me killed on the spot.

It was cloudy and gray when we arrived in Kobe. We drove through Ashiya, a wealthy neighborhood in the hills overlooking the city. It could have been a rich suburb in San Francisco or the Hollywood Hills. We passed hundreds of multimillion-dollar mansions, piled on top of each other, going up the hills, following the perfectly landscaped winding roads.

The location of the headquarters of the Hamaguma was known by practically everyone in Japan. Whenever there was a yakuza killing or a yakuza was arrested, the news reports would show a picture of the front entrance of the fortress house in Kobe, often with a yakuza spokesman making a statement.

Bao turned a corner, and we slowly drove by that same entrance. There were outdoor surveillance cameras everywhere—hung above the entrance doors and along the high stone walls that surrounded the compound, which covered an entire city block. We turned right and went down the block and then turned right again. There the wall was thirty feet tall, and we drove up to a massive black warehouse-garage door that was big enough for a semitrailer truck to drive through.

To the left of the garage was a small black door, with

a sill that was a foot off the ground and an opening four feet high and two feet across. The small door opened, and out came a very large man wearing a khaki shirt and pants, with a wide black belt and black combat boots. He had a clenched-jawed seriousness.

He walked around the front of the Toyota and opened the left-hand passenger door, and I got out. He gestured toward the small door, and Bao drove away.

CHAPTER *61*

I walked down a long, dimly lit, extremely narrow hallway. The man in the combat boots was right behind me. The hallway turned left and came out into a large formal dining room, where young yakuza recruits were clearing tables and sweeping the floor. They looked very intent on doing their work, none of them looking at me.

The guy in the combat boots motioned for me to put my hands in the air, as he thoroughly searched me from top to bottom. He pulled out the thumb drive from my right-front pants pocket. He looked at it and handed it back to me.

We walked in silence down another narrow hallway and into an expensively furnished sitting room with a carved-stone Buddha overlooking two brocade-covered couches and matching tufted, black leather armchairs.

I sat on one of the couches, looking directly at the Buddha, as the man left the room, locking the door. I waited and stared at the Buddha, trying to clear my head and calm myself.

After fifteen minutes of waiting, I got up and walked around the room. On the opposite wall was a line of ornately framed photos of what, I guessed, were the six family heads who had ruled the yakuza clan since 1915. As I was looking at the last one, the very man in the photo walked into the room alone.

This was the Sixth Kumichō, Mr. Onishi-san. He wore an expensive smooth-silk suit and rimless glasses. He bowed. I bowed. We sat across from each other on the facing couches.

He spoke impressive English, "You are a brave man coming here. You know I could make you disappear."

"Yes, you could. But if you did, some embarrassing information about you and your work for Oshima would come out. Would you like to see a sample of what we've got?"

I handed him the thumb drive. He clapped his

hands. A panel door off to the side slid open. An older man dressed in a black suit, black shirt, and black tie walked in looking like a mortician.

The *kumichō* said a few words to him in Japanese. He then turned and looked at me over the top of his glasses and said, "Would you join me for tea?"

"Yes, that would be good."

The mortician came back with a big MacBook Pro laptop and set it up on the coffee table in front of Mr. Onishi-san. He inserted the thumb drive. The screen came to life with a blast of color showing a photo of Arashi Tojo singing on stage with the two topless girls. It was followed by a series of e-mails between Tojo and senior yakuza guys in Kobe.

The *kumichō* slowly scrolled through the pages, intently reading both the ones in Japanese and English. We had edited the e-mails so that they told a story, starting with the first contact from Tojo, to the $5 million in US cash, to the killing of the players in the deception project, and to the battle at The Nam Hai. They had been encrypted on a secret server, but somehow the Hoi An hackers had found their way in.

The tea came in a white porcelain pot set on a silver

tray with two white bone-china cups and saucers. The mortician poured for both of us and silently slipped away. The *kumichō* sipped his tea and continued reading—his deadpan expression never changing, the glow of the e-mails reflected in his glasses.

After a good twenty minutes, he closed the laptop, looked at me, and said, "What do you want to do?"

I said, "I want all our problems to go away."

"How do you mean?"

"My solution is this. Instead of cleaning up Tojo's mess and killing Nachi Tanaka, why don't you clean up the real problem: Arashi Tojo himself. He double-crossed everyone who worked on the project, and now he wants her killed as the last link. You've lost men. The Hoi An police have lost men. Let's stop the killing, and we will make everything you see on your computer go away."

He looked at me and was quiet for several minutes. He pulled the thumb drive out of the computer and handed it back to me.

He said, "It is in all our interests that this episode in our history is never known. I will consider your proposal. We will be in touch with you."

I stood up. He stood up. We both bowed.

We both said, "*Sayonara*."

The guy who had searched me entered the room and escorted me through the dining area and down the narrow halls that Bao told me were designed so that in a battle, the enemy would be funneled into an area the width of one man, where the killing would be easy. My heart was thumping furiously as I stepped over the high sill of the small door and out into the cool air. I was alive. I had survived. My heart began to slow down. Bao's silver Crown sedan sat idling across the street.

I opened the door and got in. I looked at Bao and the dark circles under his eyes, which had not been there when I had first met him.

He asked, "You still got it?"

What I had was a thumb drive with a unique replicating program. It was designed so that when its contents were downloaded to a computer, it would simultaneously upload the entire memory of the computer back onto the thumb drive. I had no idea what we had. It could be everything. It could be nothing. We wouldn't know until we got back to Kyoto.

CHAPTER *62*

It was getting dark, and the streetlights were turning on as we wound our way down the hillside. The line of light cut across Kobe; the mountains put most of the city in shadow. Bao kept checking his mirrors, "I think we are being followed."

He slowed down to thirty miles per hour, and the car he was watching behind us slowed down as well and stayed about a block back. It looked like a white Honda. We came to a stoplight just before the on-ramp to the highway. The light was red, but Bao ran the intersection, flooring the car as we went up the ramp and merged with the traffic.

As I watched out the back window, it was impossible to tell in the sea of following headlights which car was the Honda. Bao was going well over one hundred miles per hour. He turned the headlights off and took the next exit without signaling or touching the brakes. We blew through another red-light intersection, took two lefts, and got back on the highway going back toward Kobe.

He got it back up to one hundred miles per hour and took an exit a couple of miles up the road. We went down the ramp and parked with our lights off on a side street in an industrial area. No white Honda came down the exit ramp. We got back on the highway for Kyoto. Every car that passed gave me a shot of paranoid fear.

CHAPTER *63*

We drove into the Ritz-Carlton's underground garage and rode the elevator up to the room where Nachi was being guarded. Hai downloaded the thumb drive. As he began scrolling through the documents, he slowly delivered the news, "I think we hit the jackpot."

There was endless evidence of thousands of crimes. Everything from murder, to extortion, to arson, to loan-sharking, to drugs, to prostitution, to bribery, to a working daily relationship with the Liberal Democratic Party—especially when a national election campaign was going on, like it was at the moment. Of course, the centerpiece of the evidence was the work for Oshima on the deception project, including Tojo's orders to have all the people involved with the project killed.

Both Oshima and the Hamaguma must have totally believed in their encryption program.

It was just like what the chairman of Nikkō had talked about in his speech to the nation, when he cited the fact that the United States had broken the JN-25 Japanese naval code in World War II. The result had been the devastating loss of four of their aircraft carriers at the Battle of Midway. Even worse, the Japanese had had no idea that the Americans had cracked their encryption system. It was a product of total arrogance and a belief that their coding system was impossible to break.

Later in the war, the United States intercepted a message that Admiral Isoroku Yamamoto, the commander in chief of the Combined Japanese Fleet and the mastermind behind the surprise attack on Pearl Harbor, was on an inspection tour of the South Pacific. The intercepted message had detailed the admiral's departure and arrival times for his trip to the Solomon Islands.

As they were preparing to land on the island of Bougainville, the Mitsubishi bomber Yamamoto was flying in, guarded by Mitsubishi Zero fighters, was attacked by a squadron of US P-38s that knew the exact time he was flying in. His plane was shot down by US fighter pilots, which proved to be a critical turning point in the war. The violence of his death was kept hidden from the Japanese public—his medical report whitewashed and changed on 'orders from above.'

In much the same way, instead of talking indirectly or in code, the yakuza made orders, had people murdered, and moved around money like they were certain their network was secure.

We suddenly had the equivalent of a nuclear device. For the next few hours, Nachi translated the e-mails and text messages. There was enough information to indict half the House of Representatives, as well as to take out the senior management of the Hamaguma family. But disturbingly, there was not one mention of the Sixth Kumichō, Mr. Onishi-san. Not a word. Not a sentence. Not a reference. It was like he wasn't running one of the largest criminal outfits in the world.

It was nearly midnight as we sat around the low, square coffee table in Nachi's living room. Each of us took a side—Bao to my right, Hai to my left, and Nachi straight ahead. The lights were low; the curtains were drawn.

I asked, "What are we going to do? If we do nothing, we might have a deal with Mr. Onishi-san. All the problems disappear. They leave us alone."

"Or they don't," Bao said. "And you continue to live your life in fear."

"But if we give the evidence up to the police, our lives won't be worth a nickel," I replied. "You think the *kumichō* won't figure it out?"

"Okay," Bao said. "So let's say the *kumichō* buys the deal: no more Arashi Tojo. We just walk away? We eat our evidence?"

"My mother is dying in a hospital, and you're going to let them go?" Nachi blurted out. "They poisoned her. You saw the e-mail. It said, 'make her sick,' and that's what happened."

"Look," Bao said. "We've just got to hunker down and wait until we hear from them. I'll see if we can get the hotel security to double the guard."

CHAPTER *64*

In the morning, we found out that Arashi Tojo had been stabbed to death in a back bedroom at the Blue Fish Hostess Club. None of the girls saw anything. He had been found by the janitors around four that morning. His attackers had slashed his throat and let him bleed to death. He was naked. It was Hitoshi Ozawa, the deputy inspector of the Tokyo Organized Crime Task Force, who called Bao with the news.

Bao said, "I think the *kumichō* may have accepted our deal."

On a side table, the phone started ringing. I picked it up. The hotel chief of security said, "Our facial-recognition software has picked up two known yakuza in our La Locanda Italian restaurant. We are watching them, but we wanted you to know in case other measures are necessary."

It was the brave new world. The hotel's facial-recognition software was tied into the Japanese national criminal database. The hotel's security knew who the yakuza guys were before they had taken their seats at the bar.

Bao sent two of his men down to the restaurant to sit with the gangsters. The hotel's security people were uniformed to look like waiters. Bao's men were doing their best to creep out the yakuza guys by silently sitting near them, drinking water.

Bao and I watched the scene going on in the restaurant in the hotel's security-office command center. It looked like a place you could launch missiles from. There were three technicians sitting at a long console, facing a wall of big video monitors. We saw one of the security guards, dressed as a waiter, serve the yakuza thugs two desserts of cheesecake topped with berries and two glasses of port—all of which they had not ordered.

Then he quietly said in Japanese, "Please enjoy with our compliments. And then we want you to leave."

One of them put an envelope on the bar with a name on it. My name on it—Christian Lindstrom. The two of them walked out. The hotel's cameras followed them down a long hallway to the motor entrance, where a black Mercedes sedan was waiting to drive them away.

The envelope had a single sheet of paper, which Nachi translated for us when it was brought upstairs. It said, "You are safe. We've done our part. Just do yours."

CHAPTER 65

We walked across the huge glass concourse of the Kyoto railroad station. It was nearly deserted, and the people who were there seemed to be swallowed up by its immense size. I walked with Hai and Nachi while Bao and his detectives fanned out around us.

We took the last express Shinkansen bullet train to Tokyo. It was raining; the train blasted through the night with stations and towns flashing by like a final good-bye. Its speed was made all the more wondrous by the fact that a bullet train had never had a fatal accident in over forty years.

It had stopped raining in Tokyo. The night air was cool and dry as we walked to the Mandarin Oriental, which was only a couple of blocks away and thirty-eight stories straight up. We sat around the dining table in Bao's suite with three laptops and began deleting all the e-mails and text messages that had anything to do with the deception project and the killings that were done for Oshima.

This was exactly what I had told the Sixth Kumichō, Mr. Onishi-san, we would do. What was left were hundreds of other crimes, including many other jobs that the yakuza had done for Oshima that had nothing to do with us, the Hoi An Massacre, or the battle at The Nam Hai.

There were records of millions in bribes that the ad agency had given the yakuza to influence the wholesalers at the Tsukiji Fish Market. There were orders for murders of politicians and people from other yakuza families, not to mention enough extortion threats to different people and their families to give me the chills as Nachi translated them for us.

For Oshima's part, there were thousands of bribes of members of the House of Representative, which were called "political contributions."

In the middle of the e-mails and PDFs, there was a terrific *Sokaiya* extortion of a manufacturer of automotive airbags. The yakuza had found out that the company was being sued by hundreds of people who had been killed and injured when the airbags had blown up in their faces.

The chairman of the company had willingly paid the yakuza $10 million in US dollars not to share the information about the lawsuits at their annual shareholders meeting.

We talked until two in the morning. Then, too tired to think, I fell asleep in a chair by the door, with Nachi in the next room.

CHAPTER **66**

For the first time, we felt safe enough to go to one of the Mandarin's restaurants for breakfast, a place called K'Shitzi. The four of us looked out at Tokyo on a perfectly cloudless, blue-sky morning, complete with Mount Fuji on the horizon. The city spread out beneath us, as miniature trains and tiny cars whizzed around thirty-eight stories below.

Nachi said, "The big question is if we are going to give the edited evidence to the police or not."

I cautioned, "I think we should quit while we are ahead. We're still alive; Tojo's dead. If the yakuza get a whiff of what we've got, they'll come at us with everything."

Bao nodded, "I think we should pack it in."

Hai said, "I must go back to Hanoi. My wife is very lonely, and my son cries for me on the phone."

"So we are decided? We end it here," I said, after several minutes of silence.

We ate breakfast, knowing this would probably be the last time we would be together, after weeks of working as a team.

We went back upstairs to pack up. Bao's detectives already had their luggage piled up in the hall. But then Nachi got a call on her cell phone from her sister, Kiki, in Kyoto. She told Nachi that someone had unplugged the ventilator that had been keeping their mother alive and that Ruri Tanaka was dead.

It was as if Nachi had been electrocuted—her agony convulsing her; her body heaving in grief. I held her and thought of her mother, who had prayed every day for the souls her grandfather had slaughtered outside of Hoi An.

Nachi cried in waves; she was totally inconsolable, shaking, heartbroken.

We had no idea how it had happened. Maybe a janitor had accidentally unplugged the ventilator. But someone had to have shut off the alarm when the power was lost.

Knowing the yakuza and their ability to terrorize, they were at the top of our list.

CHAPTER *67*

It all became a blur of sadness. We took a bullet train back to Kyoto. Nachi seemed in a trance, looking with a one-thousand-yard stare out the window as the urban landscape went rushing by.

It was all ahead of us—the wake, the Buddhist funeral, and the cremation. We took a taxi to her mother's house, where Nachi had grown up, in order to change clothes for the *tsuya*, the wake. Nachi's sister, Kiki, and her husband were there. Nachi and Kiki held each other and cried like children, as if they were never going to stop.

The wake was held at a temple high in the hills with a sweeping view of Kyoto all the way to the top of the mountains. The sky was filled with dark, low clouds moving in from the east.

There were hundreds of people I did not know. The women wore black kimonos or black dresses. The men uniformly wore black suits, with white shirts and black ties. Buddhist monks chanted a section of the *sutra*. Their voices vibrated off the temple walls, and a gong sounded softly every few seconds.

Suddenly, there was a murmur at the back of the room, as the Sixth Kumichō, Mr. Onishi-san, and his entourage walked in. They stood in a line off to the right. It was like a switch had been flipped; the atmosphere in the room changed from an enveloping sadness to something approaching terror.

Later, the *kumichō* came over and offered his sympathies to Nachi and Kiki. He tried to give Nachi a thick black-and-silver envelope of condolence money—a traditional Japanese funeral gesture. He spoke to her in a low voice. She refused to look at him or accept the money. All bets were off. I could feel our collective grief turning into a wall of rage.

The funeral and the cremation of Ruri Tanaka would take place in the morning, but that night we decided what we were going to do.

CHAPTER 68

The next evening we met with Hitoshi Ozawa, the deputy inspector of the Organized Crime Task Force of the Tokyo Metropolitan Police. It was nearly ten at night when we sat down with him in an office on the fourth floor of the hulking Tokyo police headquarters.

Bao spoke first. "As you know, we have been in your country investigating the murders yakuza members committed in Vietnam. During our time here, we have been given information that we assume was illegally obtained, but we think you may find it useful."

For the next few hours, Hitoshi Ozawa read the documents; he eventually took off his suit coat and worked in his vest. Like the *kumichō*, he read from the computer without expression, completely deadpan.

Finally he said, "This is quite extraordinary. We will need to put you under police protection. If the yakuza would kill Ms. Tanaka's mother, they could easily kill you for just entering this building, let alone talking to us."

I didn't like the way he said it. It was as if we were foolish to have come in.

"You must understand that you have handed us a very hot potato," he said with his unusual southern accent. "Even though this evidence is illegal, it will make many prosecutions possible. But more than the murders and extortions, this all goes to the very fabric of our government—our society. It is very bad news when half of the House of Representatives are on the yakuza payroll.

"But the important thing is that we get you out of Japan before we act on any of this."

Within an hour, we were saying good-bye to Hai and Bao and his detectives. They were being taken to Narita for a flight back to Hanoi and then on to Hoi An. It was very difficult. I suddenly knew how much I loved them, for their steadfast bravery and for saving our lives. I had always felt protected by Bao's determination and focus and Hai's loyalty. I felt a rush of sadness like we were saying farewell forever.

Bao said, "Please stay alert, keep a low profile, and get as far from here as you can."

I knew he meant well, but it sounded like a death sentence.

CHAPTER *69*

For our protection, Nachi and I were taken to a traditional Japanese *ryokan* guesthouse several hours outside of Tokyo. We rode through the night in a black unmarked detective's car. The darkness, not knowing where we were or exactly where we were going, fueled my fears.

Nachi said it was a well-known, secluded place for those who liked privacy and a full immersion in traditional Japanese minimalist culture. The exclusive Gora-Kadan was high in the hills, a half hour out of Kanazawa.

They gave us the Kadan Suite on the top floor, which looked out on a dense bamboo forest that rose sixty feet in the air. A balcony with a large hot-spring tub also looked out into the bamboo trees. We were given blue-and-white kimonos, and our clothes were taken away to be washed. It was three in the morning.

We lay side by side on futon mattresses holding hands in the darkness as a plainclothes policeman sat outside our door and waited for trouble.

CHAPTER *70*

I called back to my office in Boston. We had a new job scheduled in South Africa in a couple of weeks. Nachi and I decided we could fly to Cape Town and try to get the shoot moved up. Nachi tried calling the local advertising agency before she realized that it was one in the morning in Cape Town.

Deputy Inspector Ozawa arranged for Nachi's sister, Kiki, her husband, and their two kids to be relocated to an undisclosed location away from Kyoto. Nachi booked two seats on an Emirates airline flight to Cape Town, with a stop in Dubai. The Oshima credit card had stopped working, so I paid with mine and hoped that the yakuza couldn't hack into my American Express account to find out where we'd gone.

Instead of taking the bullet train back to Tokyo,

for safety, we were driven by plainclothes policemen to Narita, but we did not enter the terminal. We were driven out onto the tarmac, right up next to a massive double-decker Airbus 380—the world's largest passenger airplane.

Hustled up a stairway into a cargo hold, we climbed up another two sets of stairs and came out in the plane's upper level, in business class. We were given seats together right up against a bulkhead near the cockpit entrance, where few people would go by. But there were another 525 people aboard, and I thought about what Bao had said about staying alert and keeping a low profile.

Nachi reached for my hand and looked me straight in the eye and said, "I am so sorry for putting you through all this, Christian. Thank you for staying with me and for being my friend. I know I put all this hell in motion, but I never thought it would go like this.

"I love you. I don't want to lose you again."

For me, it was a feeling that I had experienced only once before in my life.

The engines came on to full power, and the gigantic airplane began to move, picking up speed, covering almost nine thousand feet of runway before miraculously floating into the air. It was exactly how I felt, floating in air, sitting by her side.

CHAPTER 71

Twenty-six hours later we were drinking coffee in the Bascule Bar of the Cape Grace Hotel, looking out at a Cape Town yacht harbor. Nachi had succeeded in getting the shoot rescheduled, but we still had a couple of days to ourselves.

We had been checking the Japanese news channels on the Internet, but there was nothing about the yakuza or Oshima or any of their crimes. Most of the stories were about the upcoming elections. One of the stories announced that Shiro Kobayashi, the Nikkō chairman, was running for the House of Representatives in his Osaka prefecture.

After sleeping for twelve hours, after making love like desperate people, after having a room-service breakfast in the middle of the afternoon, we got a car and driver to take us around Cape Town. We drove south toward the Cape of Good Hope. It was a cloudy, windy day, with a big surf lashing the beach at Camps Bay.

We stopped to watch a troop of baboons enjoying life by the side of the road. There were mothers with their infants, working nonstop, grooming their children and removing ticks from their fur.

Nachi looked up at me as we were nearing the Cape of Good Hope. She said, "Guess what we are?"

"What?"

"A couple."

I felt a warmth and calmness going through me like I'd had a giant shot of Demerol. When we got out of the car, we climbed the rock ramparts, looking down at the raging water of two oceans colliding. The wind and surf were so loud that we couldn't talk or hear each other, but it hardly mattered. We were a couple. The real deal.

CHAPTER 72

B ao called Nachi's cellphone at ten that night from Hoi An. Nachi put him on speaker. I was happy to hear his voice, but he was short and cryptic.

"It's five in the morning in Tokyo. It started happening about an hour ago. The BBC had part of the story—NHK World may have it all. It looks like our adversaries are reaping the whirlwind." With that, he hung up.

I wasn't sure what he meant until we tuned into the English version of a streaming NHK World television channel on the Internet. They were rousting members of the House of Representatives all over Japan, and the cops were doing it in a very rude, un-Japanese-like way.

I watched a shot of a representative in Kanazawa being dragged out of his home in his bathrobe; his hands were handcuffed behind his back. Cops on either arm hustled him into a waiting prisoner van and slammed the door behind him.

The news report cut to shots of cops in full military gear storming the Hamaguma fortress complex in Kobe. They were going over the walls using ladders. Two officers were shot while attempting to breach the small door next to the big garage. Other officers ran up and pulled them back.

But then the TV shot widened out to show a heavily armored rubber-tired Striker scout vehicle coming up the street. It turned to face the garage and the small door, and opened up with a rapid-firing 30mm cannon. Within ten seconds, the high-explosive rounds turned the garage and the small door into a pile of twisted junk. It was followed by an assault of a couple hundred pissed-off combat police swarming the newly created entrance.

It went on all day, all over the Internet and the international news channels. A dozen executives were arrested at Oshima, plus forty-two members of the House of Representatives. Another sixteen yakuza were killed in Kobe, and over one hundred more were arrested, including six of the Sixth Kumichō's top lieutenants.

In the early evening, the chairman of Oshima came on the television to announce his resignation from the agency. In an emotional apology, he cited the company culture of "Thought. Word. Deed. It placed an ultimate premium on getting results for our clients at all costs." The translation from Japanese to English subtitles gave an intensity to the gravity of his words.

"I was one who fostered this culture of willful ignorance, of looking the other way when illegal methods were used to achieve success."

Not a word was mentioned about the deception project that had brought down the government. I wondered how he could not have known what was going on.

At the same time, the Sixth Kumichō, Mr. Onishi-san, was not arrested like the members of his senior staff, whom the national police had hauled away. He was away from Kobe when the raid was launched, visiting the great seated Buddha of Kamakura. He was photographed praying at the Kōtoku-in temple at sunrise. It seemed clear that he'd been warned, and I shuddered to think what else he might know.

Nachi was crying as we watched. "Is this ever going to end? God, I hurt for my mother. I ache ... and I am responsible for her death."

There was nothing good to say. It was all in play, all in motion, and they could well be coming for us.

SPECIAL THANKS

This book would not be possible without the help of my family, friends and colleagues: **Emily Haggman,** my spectacular muse and partner; my son, **Matt Haggman,** a former Miami Herald investigative reporter, who taught me the basics of bringing a political crime story to life; **Julia Leonard,** our editor and published author (*Cold Case*, Simon & Schuster); **Melissa Cunha,** my tireless assistant and typist, who contended with my constant changes and bad handwriting; **Ann Messenger,** who designed the book cover and layout; **Mr. Shintaro Yamamoto,** for his invaluable insight and historical perspective on the New Latin Quarter and the yakuza; **Fred Collins,** the renowned photographer who did my portrait photos; **Jeanne Wallace, Alicia Crichton** and **Dawn Kenney,** our social media, digital and web team; **Redtree Productions** and **Steve Polakiewicz,** for producing our video trailer; **Nick Brown, Josh Payne, Julianna Sheridan** and **Jennifer Karin** of Matter Communications for their PR and social media work; **Nghiem Xuan Hung,** the artist who created the evocative painting on the book cover which influenced much of the story; **Tran Xuan Hai, Bich Tuyen Nguyen Thi, Yoshie Matsumoto** and **Eiko Sugimura,** our talented guides and translators in Vietnam and Japan; **Gloria Avila,** my biggest social media fan; **James Patterson,** whose Master Class inspired me to write a real thriller; and lastly, my thanks to **Jim Beardsworth** and **Andy Mendelson,** who were so kind and patient in reading *The Apology* in rough draft, filled with hundreds of nearly unreadable errors, yet offering me amazing insights, support and encouragement.

Thank you so much,

Eric